Skin Deep

Susan Inez

I hope you enjoy my
book.

Susan Inez

Llumina
Press

This book is a work of fiction. Names, characters, places, and incidents are the product of the author's imagination or are used fictitiously. Any resemblance to actual events, locales, or persons, living or dead. is coincidental.

Copyright Registration Number: TXu 1-587-581

ISBN: 978-1-60594-200-1 (Paperback)
      978-1-60594-201-8 (Hardcover)
      978-1-60594-202-5 (Ebook)

Printed in the United States of America by Llumina Press

Library of Congress Control Number: 2008909562

Dedication

First of all I would like to dedicate this novel to my grandson Ethan, my daughter Cheryl and my son Chris, who without them there would never have been inspiration for this book. I love you so much.

Acknowledgements

To my sister Jane, who never stopped believing in me or my book and has been the driving force in me finishing and publishing this book. For your faith in me I will always be grateful. Not only did God bless me with a sister but my best friend as well. I love you.

To my mama, my brother Edgar, my son-in-law Ivey, my new grandson Brandon and all my family and friends thank you for your love and support. I love you.

Thank you Tiffany so much for the book cover design. You captured exactly how I wanted it to look. You have a true gift.

Chapter One

*I*t had started out like any ordinary day for Melanie Hutchins. She had a busy day ahead, with several admissions scheduled. Melanie was an admissions nurse for the local psychiatric hospital. It was a little hospital in a small North Carolina town with only twenty beds for short term admits ranging from a few days to a few weeks. Basically, it dealt with alcohol and drug addicts needing medication adjustments and counseling, as well as those dealing with personal problems too great to bear on their own who needed evaluation and prescriptions for depression, anxiety, and other psychiatric disorders. Occasionally, a patient's behavioral problems were too much for the hospital to handle, and then the patient was transferred to Cherry Hospital in Goldsboro, NC. Cherry was a long-term psychiatric hospital equipped to handle more severe cases. Melanie thought she'd seen about every situation and heard all the excuses for drugs, alcohol, and self-destruction, but this day would prove to be one to remember.

The first admission went as usual—demographic information, medical information, social history, and a physical examination. Melanie listened carefully as the twenty-two-year-old male gave her the information she requested. She could not help but reflect on her own life and son, who only just a few months ago had admitted himself to this very hospital. Melanie then was the mother on the other side of the desk, tears streaming down her face as her son answered the very same questions. How quickly an ordinary life could be turned upside down forever.

Melanie remembered the day of the accident. She had been working the floor as a seven-to-three nurse, and had just gotten home from work. She was waiting for her friend Leona to pick her up and go to a nearby restaurant for coffee. Melanie and Leona had worked together for the last eight years. Something had clicked between them when they met, and they'd become good friends because of their lives' similarities.

The phone rang. When Melanie picked up the phone, she heard a panicked voice on the other end.

"Melanie!" the person shouted.

"Yes," Melanie answered. Whoever it was, they were calling from a cellular phone, and the reception was not clear.

"Melanie," the voice on the other end repeated anxiously.

"Yes! I'm here, but I can barely hear you!" She was still trying to recognize the panic-stricken voice on the other end of the phone.

"Kevin has been in an accident and is being flown to Pitt Hospital."

Melanie froze. "How bad is he hurt?" she asked, afraid to hear the answer. Melanie suddenly knew the voice. It was her son's mother-in-law, Lindy Jacobs.

"It's bad," Lindy's voice quivered. "He was on his motorcycle, and a car hit him."

Melanie suddenly felt weak. "I'm on my way."

Melanie's daughter-in-law had called her mom to come immediately and asked that Lindy get in touch with Kevin's family. Lindy was already on the road to Greenville when she called. Melanie hung up the phone and dialed Leona, who was still at work. She told Leona what had happened and asked her to come immediately. Melanie then called Kevin's dad to tell him. When Dan answered the phone, his voice said he already knew. He, too, was leaving to go to the hospital. He had their daughter Morgan with him, and he said they would meet her at the hospital.

Melanie tried to focus on the young man in front of her. What was it this time? Drugs? Alcohol? What breaks the spirit of such a handsome young man? Can we help him? God, I hope so, she prayed.

He wouldn't look at her when he answered her questions. Instead, he looked at his hands, which were fidgeting in his lap. His blonde, curly hair fell in his face as he looked down. He was slim, about 5'10". He looked like Bo Duke, from *Dukes of*

Hazard. He really was cute. It was a shame his life was so messed up. Jason Pearce was his name, and for now, she did not know why he was here. Melanie tried not to become too attached to her patients, something she had been taught from her early days at nursing school.

"Keep an open mind and don't let your feelings interfere with your decisions and good judgment." But Melanie had learned that was a hard thing to do. She was a caring, compassionate person, and it was easy for her to cross that fine line. She wanted to care about every patient she met, and she did become too attached sometimes.

Melanie noticed the sad, lost look on Jason's face and wondered why there were no family members present. Did he have any family?

When she finished the paperwork, Jerry, the male nurse, took Jason to show him his room and get him settled in. Jerry would do a physical search to make sure there were no drugs hidden in his clothes or on his body. Dr. Williams, the facility medical director and lead physician, would be notified of Jason's arrival and admission.

Melanie only lived a few blocks from the hospital, so she usually ran home for lunch. While she was home, she checked her messages. No messages, these days, was good news. It meant everything was okay for another day. Melanie returned to work at one p.m., ready for her second admission.

She was surprised when the admission arrived. It was an attractive older lady. Her name was Scarlet. She had almost-black hair with just a touch of gray and an olive complexion. Her skin was smooth and had very few wrinkles, even though she was in her early sixties. She must have been really beautiful at one time. She was still quite striking. Scarlet's eyes were made up, and her lips were painted just right to compliment her natural beauty.

Scarlet spoke softly, just like a southern bell. It was easy to tell she was well educated. She had been an RN for thirty years, she told Melanie proudly. Melanie could just picture her in a crisp white uniform and white cap. She probably turned a lot of heads in her time.

Melanie listened as Scarlet answered her questions, volunteering more information than was requested. She was anxious to talk, or maybe she was just nervous. Melanie had already decided she liked Scarlet. She respected her, even though she had just met her a few moments ago. Scarlet had class. Pure and simple.

Scarlet began to ask Melanie questions. "Do you have children?"

"Yes," Melanie answered.

"How old are they?" Scarlet asked.

Melanie told Scarlet she had a twenty-four-year-old son and a nineteen-year-old daughter. Scarlet's eyes brightened briefly, and she gave Melanie a big smile. Scarlet told Melanie that she'd had a son, but he'd been killed when he was twenty-four.

"That was eighteen months ago," she said sadly. Her mood suddenly dropped.

Melanie couldn't help but feel sad for the lady in front of her. She said she could only imagine how awful that must have been, for she, too, had come close to losing her son in a motorcycle accident three years ago.

Scarlet's eyes widened. "My son was sitting on his motorcycle beside the road when a truck struck him. The motorcycle was knocked out from under him and hardly damaged at all. However, my son was hit in the head, declared brain dead at the hospital, and died two days later."

Melanie suddenly thought of how blessed she was that her son had been spared. She had always believed there was a reason her son had survived. She felt God had given her time to renew her relationship with her son. Things had needed to be said that hadn't been, and God had been generous to give them a chance to mend the relationship damaged by her and Dan's divorce. Kevin's wife hadn't helped matters. She was jealous of his family, his friends, and everything he cared about. She wanted to be his whole life. In other words, she was a control freak.

Scarlet talked about her son until she became too emotional to continue. Melanie handed her a tissue and shifted the conversation back to her admission information. After a few moments, Scarlet was able to continue. Melanie asked for next of kin.

Scarlet shook her head. "I only have friends, no next of kin. I had a husband, but he took up with my best friend when I had an emotional break down after my son was killed. That's when I said to hell with husbands and to hell with best friends," she said, throwing both arms up in disgust.

Melanie could understand why Scarlet suffered from severe depression. Losing her son, her husband, and her best friend. Who wouldn't be depressed?

Melanie finished her paperwork and took Scarlet to her room. Leona came in to do a nursing assessment and a physical check. Leona began to ask Scarlet her medical history. As Melanie left, she gave Scarlet a little wave, and Scarlet smiled and waved back.

"Not again," Melanie said under her breath as she walked away, already attached to the new patient. "My heart can't take any more." She shook her head. "I won't get emotionally involved. I won't! Not this time."

Melanie left work thinking about her new admissions, especially Scarlet and Jason. It had been an interesting day, to say the least. Both reminded her of her own life in a strange sort of way. She threw in a microwave dinner, changed into something more comfortable, and checked the answering machine again. There was a message from Jill Roberts.

"Hi, Melanie; this is Jill. Give me a call first chance you get. Bye."

She barely knew Jill, but she had bumped into her and her husband Ray in Wal-Mart a couple of Saturday nights in a row and had randomly struck up a conversation. Ray asked Melanie if she was seeing anyone. She told him she occasionally had a dinner date with a friend of a friend, but it was just a friendship, not a relationship.

Ray and Jill spoke at once. "We have been talking about you to a friend of ours, and we want to get the two of you together."

Melanie had laughed. She had been fixed up on a couple of other blind dates before. Her sister Joan had once arranged a date with the assistant pastor of her church. "Nice guy," Joan had said. Well, the nice guy had wanted to take her home with him on the first date. He had also had a foot fetish. He wanted to see if her toenails were painted to match her fingernails.

No, thank you, Melanie had thought about Jill's proposition. But she smiled and said,

"Sure, I'd like that."

They had seemed happy she had agreed and said they would try to arrange a get-together soon.

Melanie didn't put a whole lot of stock in this being any different from the other let-downs. She didn't rush to call back and arrange a meeting. Instead, she ate her microwave dinner and thought over the idea.

What's wrong with this life? No hassle, no fussing, no fighting—no one to love. Melanie had decided that loving no one was much better than loving the wrong one. She had certainly been down that road with James Parker. No fun there—just a lot of heartache and pain. She was glad she had finally been able to break that hold and end the relationship. Again, God had answered her prayers in a strange sort of way.

Melanie had prayed that if she couldn't leave James alone he would resist her to the point that she would have to eventually give up and go on without him. That is exactly what happened. She approached him several times after they broke up, and he wanted nothing to do with her. God had done it again. He had saved her sanity, maybe even her life. The relationship was not a good one. She had started dating James soon after her separation. He was so different from her husband, to whom she had been married for twenty years. He was fun, exciting, and dangerous. A little on the wild side. Melanie had never been to dances, never drunk alcohol, and lived a very boring life. At least, that's what she thought for a while. It was all new to her. It was exciting; it was fun to feel alive. He turned out to be worse than her ex-husband. At least her ex didn't physically abuse her.

Dan was really a nice guy—to everyone but his wife and kids. They could never live up to his expectations. Melanie had developed really low self-esteem and so had her children. He embarrassed her and her son in front of their friends by putting them down then laughing like it was some sort of joke.

Everyone thought he was a great person, always ready to lend a helping hand to those who needed it, and he was; he just didn't know how to make his own family feel worthy. Maybe she needed more affection than a lot of women. Melanie wasn't sure, but she always felt she didn't measure up to what Dan wanted or expected.

She tried not to judge people by rumors because one never knew what went on behind closed doors. People looked for love where they could find it. Sometimes it wasn't always in the right place, as Melanie had learned the hard way, and sometimes it was where you least expected it, as Melanie would eventually find out. As for James, that was a story she preferred to forget. He had a violent temper and lived for himself. Everything had to be his way. He was another control freak. She was thankful the relationship had ended and she had survived it.

Melanie sometimes felt it would be nice to have a male friend with no attachments. Someone to do things with, but not to be involved with romantically. She wondered if there was such a thing. There should be.

Leona said it wasn't possible, that at some point, you would cross the line, and the relationship would change. She felt all men wanted to be physically involved, even if not romantically involved. In other words, they wanted to have sex. She was probably right. But Melanie still dreamed of having a guy friend without ties and without having to sleep with him. Leona said the only way for that to happen was to find a gay guy to be a friend. Still, Melanie hoped to meet the perfect male friend one day—just to be a friend, a buddy, a confidant. It could happen. Maybe, somewhere out there, a man was looking for a female friend with no romantic attachments. That could be her. She wasn't giving up on the idea just yet.

Melanie returned to work the next day to find Scarlet waiting for her in the lobby that joined her office.

"I was waiting for you," Scarlet said with a big smile.

"You were?" Melanie answered cheerfully.

Again, Melanie felt the connection. A strange closeness. It was like meeting someone for the first time, but feeling as if you had known them all your life. Scarlet put her arms out for a hug. Melanie was surprised, but she accepted the hug as she would from any friend. Melanie opened her office and Scarlet followed, taking a seat in front of Melanie's desk. Melanie sat in the chair across from her.

"I want to tell you more about my son," Scarlet said.

Melanie smiled. "I'd like that," she said.

"His name was Bryan. Bryan Adam Lane. He was named after my father and looked just like him—his smile, his gentle personality, even his laugh," Scarlet said, smiling.

Scarlet pulled a picture out of her purse to show Melanie. Melanie looked at the picture and saw her son with dark, wavy hair. He favored Scarlet, with his dark hair and olive complexion. He was a handsome young man, Melanie thought.

"He was very good looking," Melanie said, uncomfortable that Scarlet's son was dead.

"He was a jeweler," Scarlet said proudly. "He designed these two rings just for me."

Scarlet held her hands out so Melanie could see the rings. They were beautiful. He obviously was quite talented. Melanie smiled, still sad for Scarlet's loss. It was obvious she'd loved her son very much.

"Was he married?" Melanie asked.

Scarlet's smile faded. "Yes, he was."

Melanie sensed there was not much love there. She could certainly relate to that. She heard a commotion outside her office at the nursing station. She stepped out to see what was going on. It was Jason. He was upset about something and cursing at the nurse about his breakfast not being right. He had wanted eggs. They had sent him pancakes. The nurse tried to calm him, but he would not quiet down. Melanie walked a little closer, thinking maybe she could help calm him down. She had been through this same sort of thing with her son. She told Jason it was okay, that the staff would be told not to send him pancakes from now on. Just as quickly as he had blown up, he calmed down.

"Okay," he said.

"That's all I want. Eggs. Not pancakes," he said calmly.

"Okay," Melanie said. "No problem."

Jason walked back to his room, shaking his head, but he didn't say anything else.

When Melanie returned to her office, Scarlet was gone. She sat at her desk, leaned back in her chair and reflected on how her son had behaved out-of-character since his accident. His temper would flare up at nothing, and he would get angry so easily.

Just before his admission to the psych hospital, he had been fired from his job for cursing at his boss over a minor misunderstanding. It had been so ugly they had barred him from the premises. The owner had been really upset about having to fire Kevin because he had worked so hard and gotten along with everyone, until all of a sudden, his personality started changing.

He had been so different since the accident. He used to be the class clown at school and was always in trouble with the teachers for acting up. He had a love/ hate relationship with them. They really loved him, but pretended to hate his cutting up. He used to love to tease her and make her laugh and he loved hiding behind the door and saying, "Boo." She always screamed. It was just a little boo, but she always hollered, and he always laughed. Once, he was on the phone and told his friend to listen when she came in the back door. Kevin said, "Boo," and sure enough, she hollered, and he and his friend both got a kick out of it.

He was a fun-loving guy with a great smile and dimples. All the girls thought he was good-looking. Unfortunately, of all the girls he could have chosen, he chose the woman from hell. The one with the demon living in her soul. Melanie hated that she felt this way, but others thought the same thing.

How could anyone with a heart set out to destroy her husband's relationships with his family and friends? Kevin had started to withdraw from his family and friends shortly after his marriage to Rhonda. Melanie first thought, well, he's just busy, but he started acting so different that she became worried about him. When she mentioned the changes to Rhonda, his wife became angry and defensive. At one point, she even told Melanie to back off or she would be sorry. It was actually a threat. It only made Melanie more determined to find out the truth. Why did he speak in a whisper when she talked with him on the phone? Why did he distance himself from a sister that he had always been close to? Why did he stop coming home to visit? And why did he not carry on a conversation, but only answer yes or no questions in a voice she could barely hear?

Melanie and her ex had very different opinions of the situation. Her ex thought, of course, the way he always thought, negatively, that it was drugs. Melanie, on the other hand, thought it was depression. They had argued many times on the phone about the situation and what to do about it. Melanie ended up in tears most of the time, totally frustrated. They had never been able to agree on anything, and things hadn't changed, even though they were divorced.

Dan always assumed the worse and couldn't be convinced otherwise. Melanie felt all the signs pointed to depression. The withdrawal from family and friends, his whispered answers and inability to look at someone talking to him—much like Jason. Her thoughts of Jason brought her back to the present.

Melanie was due to sit in on a conference meeting with Jason, Dr. Williams, Leona—who was the director of nursing—and Rebecca, the social worker this afternoon. She was part of a care plan team that met with the patients and worked towards a plan of care for their time at the hospital, as well as a plan of care for when they were discharged. The team tried to connect the patients with outside resources that could make a huge difference in their lives if they would take advantage of the help offered. Melanie hoped Jason would let them help him. She also hoped his parents would show up to support him.

Chapter Two

*I*t was finally the weekend. Melanie and Leona usually ate breakfast together on Saturday mornings. Melanie looked forward to it. Leona was a good friend and one of the most caring and compassionate people she had ever known. She had chosen the right career when she chose to be a nurse. Her loving personality was a gift to her patients. Unfortunately, life had not smiled on Leona in relation to her love life, either. She had been unhappily married to a selfish dictator for twenty-five years before finally saying enough and getting out of the marriage. She, too, had fallen victim to the single life of fun and excitement for a while. She, too, later realized it was not the life she wanted. Again, the similarities in their lives were unbelievable.

It was like a reflection in a mirror when they compared their past, often with tears, and occasionally a laugh. Both regretted what disrupting their homes had done to their children and shared the guilt of those circumstances. Melanie had often wondered if she had not left home if things would have turned out differently. Her ex had tried to destroy the respect her children had for her, and she felt he had done some damage. She prayed she could one day make it up to them and hoped they would eventually understand her decision to leave their father.

Ted's Diner was busy with its regulars. The small, family-owned restaurant offered hometown hospitality and a familiarity everyone loved. Customers knew the owner, the waitresses, and even the cooks and visited with one another from table to table. They never knew who was going to walk by and just sit down at the table with them and start talking. That's what Melanie liked about this small town, even though it also meant everybody knew everybody's business, which could be a pain sometimes. Nevertheless, she preferred it over the big cities, where nobody cared. Unfortunately, people here were set in some old-fashioned ways that Melanie did not care for. Maybe she, too, had shared these ways at one time, but more and more, as time and circumstances pulled at her old beliefs, she saw how narrow-minded they were. She knew, though, that many people here would never change the way they felt about certain things, such as racial beliefs. Even with changing times, there were still a lot of prejudiced people in this town. You might say the small town had never grown up; it remained the same, unchanged by current events.

Many whites were prejudiced against blacks, and many blacks were prejudiced against whites. They worked together like heroes, but after work, they each went to their corners and didn't look for each other until they were at work again; then they could be friends and co-workers. That's just the way it was here. A handful of people had seen the light, but not many, and the ones that did pretty much kept it quiet, much like Melanie. She preferred not to make waves, so she never verbalized her true feelings on racial issues. She stayed neutral.

Melanie's ex had told her that their daughter Morgan had been seen riding in a car with a black boy. He was furious. He had talked ugly to Morgan and threatened to take her car if he found out it was true. Of course, Morgan denied it. Melanie thought if it was true, he was just a friend. Morgan had lots of black friends. She played sports in high school and was home-coming queen her senior year. Morgan loved people, regardless of their race. Everyone knew she was genuine and did not let color affect her feelings towards someone. She treated everyone equal, and everybody liked her. Morgan always had a smile and a good word for everybody she met.

Melanie tasted the hot coffee and told Leona about the pos-sibility of a blind date with a friend of some friends she had met. Melanie had sort of stalled on the blind date deal, but it was time to try again. Leona encouraged her to go through with it. Melanie decided to call this afternoon and see if her friends could arrange a meeting this weekend. She was glad she had finally decided to take another chance, but she did not have big expectations.

After breakfast, Melanie and Leona went to Smithfield to the Outlet Mall to spend the day together. It was always relaxing to get away from house and yard work. Most of the time, if one of them said she needed to be home cleaning, the other could easily convince her that shopping would be much more fun than spending the day cleaning. Life was too short for all work and no play. Nursing could be stressful, not to mention all the other complicated things going on in their lives. They needed R&R on Saturdays.

On the way home that afternoon, Melanie mentioned the blind date again, and after several moments of encouragement from Leona, Melanie picked up the cell phone and called Jill to see if they might be up to the four of them meeting for coffee later on that night. Jill answered the phone, excited that Melanie had called. They agreed to meet at seven p.m. at a local restaurant. Okay, it was done; she was actually going through with it. Surprisingly, she looked forward to it.

After Leona left, Melanie repaired her makeup and brushed her hair. She looked in the mirror and thought of all the reasons he shouldn't find her attractive—fat (not really, she weighed 135 pounds); old and wrinkled (she looked ten years younger than her real age of forty-two); gray hair (it was blonde). It was the same old story. She lowered her self-esteem until she felt unworthy of anybody loving her. Why would anyone love her? she thought, looking in the mirror.

"Crazy! It's just a date, not a proposal."

She laughed at herself for even thinking about the possibility of love. She hadn't met the man yet, so why was she worried about her impression on him? Besides, if it was like the rest of her blind dates, he would be the one that got dumped after the first date, not her.

She arrived at the restaurant fifteen minutes early, a little nervous. They were already there when she walked in. Jill waved, and she walked over to the booth where they were sitting. An attractive man sat alone on one side of the booth. He stood as she approached, and Jill's husband Ray introduced them. Melanie liked what she saw, which was already an improvement over all the other blind dates she'd had in the past. She sat down in the booth next to Ron.

Ronald Whitley was his name. He owned and ran his own computer business in a nearby town. The four talked for hours. They were all about the same age and had many stories about growing up in the area. Melanie relaxed and enjoyed her new friend's company. She liked him. She couldn't believe he didn't have a huge nose or big ears or something wrong with him. So far, she didn't see anything she didn't like. It was a miracle, she thought to herself. I actually like this guy. He appeared to be enjoying her company, as well.

At ten p.m., the restaurant closed. The pitfalls of a small town. Everything closed at ten o'clock. Townspeople teased that they even rolled the sidewalks up at ten. Everyone said how much they had enjoyed the evening, and Jill and Ray left to go home. Ron walked Melanie to her car and said he had enjoyed meeting her and would like to see her again some time if it was okay. Melanie smiled and said she would like that. Ron kissed her goodbye on the cheek. Melanie thought that was sweet and innocent enough. She felt good about the whole night. It had been unusually nice. She hoped he would call and ask her out again.

Chapter Three

On Monday morning, Melanie learned the weekend had not been so smooth at the hospital. Jason had gotten into a couple of encounters with the staff and had threatened them. Security had to be called in to calm him down. Why was he so angry? Melanie hoped he got better, or he would end up being sent to Cherry Hospital for treatment. Leona had worked the floor over the weekend and was concerned for Jason's well being. Leona, too, had a son close to Jason's age with problems with depression. He had used alcohol and drugs as his own treatment. Leona worried about Jason and hoped his family would show up soon to support him.

Family support was one of the biggest tools a person had in recovery. Without it, it was ten times harder after being discharged from Eastside to stay clean and out of trouble.

Melanie saw Jason sitting alone in front of the big-screen TV in the shared recreational room. He was looking at the TV, but didn't seem to be seeing it. He was deep in thought and in a world all his own. Melanie decided to talk with him for a few moments. She sat down beside him and spoke gently, so as not to startle him. He turned to look at her, but had little expression on his face. She knew he would rather be left alone. Nevertheless, she pursued a conversation, in hopes of cheering him up. No sooner had she started to talk than Scarlet came and sat down beside her.

Scarlet was her usual talkative self. Melanie couldn't help but admire her. There was something about her that was attractive and likeable. She was such a friendly, loving soul you couldn't help but like her. Again, she mentioned her son and showed Jason the rings he had made her. Jason appeared uninterested, but did turn his head to look at the rings. One ring had three stones in it. One was a diamond, for the month of April, which happened to be Scarlet's birthstone. Very appropriate for such a fine lady. The diamond was in the middle, sitting just above the other two stones. One outside stone was an emerald, for the month of May, representing her son's birthday. Melanie's son had also been born in May. The other stone was a ruby, for the month of July, representing her husband's birthday. It indeed was a beautiful ring.

The ring on her left hand was a cluster of diamonds and sapphires, equally beautiful. It was obvious that her son had been a talented jeweler. But what made them so precious to Scarlet was the fact that her son had made them for her. He had given her the birthstone ring on her sixtieth birthday. The other he had given her on Mother's Day, two months before he was killed.

Melanie got up to go to her office and left Scarlet on the sofa with Jason. Scarlet continued to talk about God knows what, but Jason never spoke to her. She didn't seem bothered by that fact and continued to smile and talk to him for a while longer then she strolled back to her room, speaking to everyone she met. Scarlet seemed happy, but Melanie knew the pain she carried in her heart. She also knew that at times, Scarlet would hardly talk at all and was so depressed she would not come out of her room for days. Melanie could relate. She'd suffered overwhelming stress that made her question everything—wondering where she went wrong with her marriage, her kids, and even her being. Melanie thought about her beautiful daughter.

When Melanie and her husband separated, Morgan was fifteen years old. Melanie left Morgan with her father so she could continue going to the same school and graduate with the same group of friends that she had started kindergarten with. Melanie lay in bed at night after leaving home and cried for her daughter and the hole left in her heart after breaking up her family. She did not know then that the guilt would be ten-fold the price she felt her children paid for her mistakes.

Melanie was brought back to the present when Dr. Williams knocked on her door and reminded her of Jason's care plan meeting in fifteen minutes. Melanie took her notebook, grabbed a fresh cup of coffee, and headed to the conference room.

Leona, also on the care plan team, was already going over notes to discuss with the rest of the group. Melanie and Leona took the time alone to talk before the rest of the group came in. They could tell each other anything and have it remain confidential, and it seemed there was always something they needed to tell each other. They took moments like these to catch up.

"Have you heard from Ron?" Leona asked with a smile.

"No," Melanie answered.

"Well, you will. Just give it some time," reassured Leona.

About that time, Dr. Williams, Rebecca, and Jerry walked into the room. The ladies hushed, as if they had been discussing underground secrets that would affect the world.

Dr. Williams, a well known psychiatrist, was tall and lanky and had a reputation for telling it like it is. He used the word "Damn" a lot, but he said it so calmly that it didn't sound like a cuss word. It almost sounded like everyday language, and to Dr. Williams, it was everyday language. Most people liked and respected him. Melanie had never heard anyone say anything bad about him, except for his colorful language and his knack for being so honest that he sometimes offended people. Melanie thought he was downright handsome and sexy, even in his mid-sixties.

Dr. Williams looked over the notes that staff had been making on Jason. It seemed that Jason had been in trouble quite a few times. Jason's mother had killed his alcoholic father when he was twelve to protect her family.

"Wow," Melanie thought. "No wonder he's messed up. Poor Jason."

After some discussion about Jason's past, Dr. Williams asked Jerry to get Jason. As Jason entered the conference room, everyone could tell he was going to have an attitude, big time. They were right. Jason was not very pleasant. Melanie couldn't help but feel that maybe he was intimidated by so many strangers prying into his personal life. She wished he understood that they only wanted to help him. Jason sat in a swiveling office chair and nervously kept the chair moving. He didn't look directly at anyone. He answered Dr. Williams' questions with as little information as possible. Dr. Williams explained that he was there to help him, not judge him. Jason made no comment. The meeting lasted about forty-five minutes, and maybe a little of the ice on Jason's heart had been chipped away, although there was no sign of it today. Melanie hoped he would allow them to enter into the world he kept to, but that would ultimately be up to him.

Chapter Four

$\mathcal{M}$elanie headed home after an emotionally tiring day and checked her messages. There were none. She had only been home a short while when Morgan came home. Morgan had moved in with Melanie after she graduated from high school. She was taking a class at the community college to get her CNA license and working at her aunt's Christian book store part-time for spending money.

Morgan had originally started nursing school, but she'd decided it was not for her and dropped out. Melanie knew unless her daughter truly wanted to be a nurse, she would never make it through the long, sleepless hours and hard work. She finally gave up trying to make Morgan see the light. For now, Morgan seemed happy with what she was doing. Working at the store gave her the opportunity to meet a lot of people. She often came home and told Melanie about the people she met and what had interested her about them or their lives.

"I need you to help me move the furniture around so we can put up the Christmas tree," Melanie said.

Morgan had already kicked off her shoes and plopped down on the couch. She didn't move.

"Come on. Help me."

Morgan didn't move.

Again, Melanie urged her daughter to help her, hoping she would catch some of the Christmas spirit she was beginning to feel. She loved Christmas and enjoyed putting up the tree and decorating the house.

"I can't," Morgan grunted, half under her breath.

"Come on. I need your help. I can't move the couch by myself," Melanie pleaded playfully.

"I'm not lifting anything heavy," Morgan said, avoiding eye contact.

"Come on, don't be a wimp," Melanie said, laughing.

"No! I can't. I told you!"

"Oh, that time of month, huh?" Melanie asked, wincing in sympathy.

"No! It's not that time of month," Morgan answered sarcastically.

Melanie didn't understand, but then, sometimes you just couldn't figure out your kids. That was nothing new. "Well, then, come on and help me; it'll only take a minute. I'll do most of the pulling and lifting if you're not feeling well."

"I'm not lifting anything heavy," Morgan said loudly.

"Why? Did you hurt your back or something?" Melanie asked, getting concerned.

"No. Just stop asking me to help," Morgan answered, annoyed.

Melanie was confused. "Have I done something to make you angry?"

"No, I just can't lift anything heavy and I told you two times already," Morgan said, getting tired of the third-degree.

Melanie's mind started to whirl, and her smile vanished as she stared at Morgan. "Why not?"

"I'm just not," Morgan said firmly.

Melanie felt something between sick and fear. "Why not?" she repeated, louder.

Morgan continued avoiding eye contact and said nothing.

Melanie knew the answer, but hoped she was mistaken. "Please tell me you aren't insinuating what I think."

"I'm not saying anything," Morgan answered stiffly.

"Oh, yes, you are. I have a right to know. You live in my house, and I want to know the truth."

Melanie did not want to say the word, in case she was reading something wrong. She didn't want to hurt Morgan's feelings if she was wrong, but some things a woman just knows. Finally, Melanie couldn't stand it any longer. "Are you pregnant?"

Morgan looked at Melanie, and the tears started to roll down her face. "Yes," she whispered. She looked down in shame.

Melanie collapsed on the couch in disbelief. What on earth could happen next to complicate her life? Divorce, her son's brain injury, and now her unmarried daughter was pregnant. Melanie didn't even know who the father was. Her mind went crazy with questions. Morgan wasn't really dating anyone. She had broken up with her long-time boyfriend Marcus months ago, and was just hanging out with friends, or so Melanie thought. Oh, my God! Her mind raced back. She prayed as hard as she could, thinking of the possibilities. She remembered what Dan had said about Morgan being seen with a black boy.

"It couldn't be. She wouldn't," Melanie assured herself. She feared the worse, but prayed she was wrong. Maybe she and Marcus had gotten together for a last hoorah before he left for college.

"Who is the father?" Melanie asked stiffly.

No answer.

"Who is the father?" she demanded again, almost yelling. "Who, Morgan?"

Melanie was getting hotter by the minute. Her heart was racing and her face was red with rage. She was tired of the guessing games. She had never been as angry or frustrated with Morgan as she was at this moment. She had to pull everything out of her, and it was really ticking her off.

"Just tell me, damn it, Morgan. Who is the daddy? Is it Marcus?"

"No!" Morgan answered quickly.

"Do you even know who the daddy is?" Melanie shouted angrily, knowing Morgan was not that kind of girl, but she was angry now, and words were flying out of her mouth without her thinking how they sounded.

Morgan stared at her irate mother in disbelief. "Yes, I know who the father is!"

"Is he black?" Melanie demanded. There, the word was out. Melanie stared at Morgan, waiting for the answer.

Morgan cried, dreading the inevitable confrontation. She knew it would be a shock and a disgrace, and that part of it she hated. "I'm not going to have an abortion. That's why I didn't tell you sooner," she said hesitantly.

"Morgan, is the father black?" Melanie asked, feeling the heat rise in her face.

"Yes, he is black," Morgan admitted, finally looking Melanie in the eyes, bracing for what came next. Tears rolled down Morgan's face, but she was ready.

Melanie felt like the whole world had just fallen on her shoulders—again. She was stunned. She dropped to the couch that had started the whole conversation. Morgan's defensiveness faded. She began to plead with her mother not to tell her father. She knew the scene would be horrific. She was correct about that.

Melanie felt anger and pity for her daughter. She loved Morgan with all the breath in her body, but for the life of her couldn't understand why she would allow this to happen.

Morgan looked at Melanie through tear-glazed eyes and whispered, "I wanted something of my own to love that loved me."

"I love you, your daddy loves you, we all love you," cried Melanie, still angry at Morgan for her betrayal of trust and all the uproar her pregnancy would cause family and friends.

"It's not the same. I wanted something all my own to love and to love me back, no matter what."

Did divorce cause this? Should she have been paying more attention, rather than worrying about her own happiness? Maybe I did do this, thought Melanie. Maybe if I'd been a better mother, my son wouldn't be hurt and my daughter wouldn't need a baby to love her. Was Morgan looking for something she hadn't found in her own life? Was my ex right about our son and drugs? Was he also a victim of a broken home, a bad mother? Maybe if she hadn't left home, none of this would have happened. She would have been paying closer attention to what was going on with Morgan. Melanie sighed and shook her head then got off the sofa, went to the loveseat, and put her arms around her daughter. They cried together for a few minutes before either said another word.

Then Morgan said, "Don't tell Daddy yet!"

Melanie didn't answer, but she was in no hurry to invite disaster, either. She didn't know how she would ever approach him with this. She didn't know how she would approach any of her family with this. Even some of her friends would be a problem, and she knew it.

Melanie would stand by her daughter. She had always tried to be there to pull her children up whenever they fell. Now was no different, but inside, Melanie was beginning to feel she could hardly pull herself up anymore.

"Does the father know he is about to become a daddy?" asked Melanie.

"Yes, he wants the baby. He doesn't want me to have an abortion."

As hard as the road ahead would be, Melanie did not want her daughter to have an abortion, either. She had always believed life was a gift from God and a blessing. Somewhat ashamed of herself, Melanie wondered what about this could possibly be a blessing—unmarried mother, biracial child in a small southern town where interracial relationships were looked down on by both races.

"Oh, God, please help us," she said quietly, out loud. Melanie again enveloped Morgan in her arms as Morgan cried softly, fearing what lay ahead for her and her baby.

Melanie would not turn her back on Morgan. She would be there for her, as she always had, even though this was topping the scale of her strength and faith. A wave of helplessness filled her body. How would they ever survive this? Tears rolled down her face as she hugged Morgan closer. How?

Chapter Five

It was almost Christmas, and Melanie had mixed feelings of Christmas cheer and reality dread. Every time she started feeling a little happy, reality kicked in, and all her problems knocked her spirit back down again. She had not shared her daughter's secret with anyone yet, not even Leona. She knew Leona would be okay with it, but she had not wanted to talk about it. Not just yet. She had to accept the fact and face it. Some of her friends would not accept the situation and wondered how it would affect her relationship with them, but her daughter would always come first. Concerned about the future, she thought about the scripture "For we walk by faith, not by sight." (2 Corinthians 5:7) It was out of her hands. She could only pray for guidance in handling what lay ahead.

Melanie knew her family would stand by Morgan, no matter how difficult it was. Her family had always been there for her, and she knew they would be this time, also. She dreaded telling them, just the same. She would tell Joan first because they'd always shared that sister closeness, and she knew Joan would support Morgan. There was no question that Charles and Carol would also be supportive, as would her parents. It wasn't that she feared they wouldn't be supportive; she just felt it would disappoint them. And why wouldn't it? Morgan was a smart, beautiful girl with her whole future ahead of her. They all wanted the best for her. She would have to tell them soon, but she felt it would be best to wait until after Christmas.

At work, the hospital was decorated for Christmas. A Christmas tree in the corner of the recreation room was covered in colored decorations the residents and staff had made, making it much more special. A popcorn chain hung loosely around the tree, giving it a homier look than store-bought decorations. Pictures of residents and staff glued onto snowflakes made it look like a tree the Waltons might have had. It was actually very attractive. On top was an angel with a broken wing. How appropriate, Melanie thought. Just like some of the people here—not just the residents, but the people taking care of the residents, including herself. Sometimes Melanie felt like she had a broken wing, and no matter how hard she tried to fly, she always fell back to the ground. She shook the thought, not wanting to get too deep into her soul.

A scream startled her back from her thoughts. It sounded like someone dying. It was a loud cry that spoke not of physical hurt, but an emotional one. It came from Scarlet, in her room.

"My rings! My rings are gone! They're missing from my nightstand!" she cried.

Tears ran down her face, and she bent over like someone in pain. She fell to her knees and put her face in her hands. Her body writhed as she wept. "My son made those rings for me, and they are gone, just like him. Taken from me for no reason, without any warning."

She was so distraught it was hard to understand her. She continued weeping, as if her heart was broken. The rings had given her the comfort of having a part of him with her all the time, and now she didn't even have that. Melanie was stunned. Tears started to run down her face. She quickly wiped them back, but they kept coming. She went to Scarlet, put her arms around her, and helped her to her feet.

Scarlet leaned on her as if she had no energy to even support her own body. Melanie helped her sit on the bed, put her arms around Scarlet, and slowly rocked back and forth as she used to do with her children when they were upset. Scarlet cried helplessly, like someone whose heart was breaking.

Melanie didn't know what to say, except, "We'll find them; I promise you."

As she spoke, anger filled her body. She meant what she had just said. She would find the rings. Who in their right mind would do such a thing to such a sweet woman? No one with even the smallest conscience could do such a thing to a woman that always had something nice to say to everyone. She was the one shining light in this whole place.

Leona brought Scarlet some medicine to help calm her down. Scarlet swallowed the medication with no questions and no resistance.

"All I ever wanted was for my son to grow up, get married, and have children of his own. Grandchildren. I didn't even get to have a grandchild, someone to call me Grandma—someone to spoil and rock to sleep at night, someone to hug me and give me butterfly kisses on the cheek, someone to teach ABCs, count, read fairytales, and teach Bible stories to. In a grandchild, I could see my son all over again and have the same joys that I had with him as a child. Instead, I have an empty life. No one to love or to love me. I feel cheated." She wept uncontrollably, and Melanie held Scarlet close, trying to console her.

Melanie thought about her daughter and the child she was carrying. The one that would soon be her grandchild. Suddenly, she began to think of the baby as a person, a real little human being that would call her "Grandma" and love her like no one else ever would. Suddenly, she felt a throb in her heart. For the first time, she felt love for her unborn grandchild.

Melanie stayed with Scarlet until the older woman fell asleep then tiptoed out of the room and pulled the door to behind her. Staff was already in a meeting discussing the theft and how to handle the situation. A grievance report had to be filed, and staff and residents would all be questioned. They had to find those rings, or Scarlet would never have any peace of mind again. It was almost like losing her son all over again. They had to find those rings.

Chapter Six

*M*elanie went home depressed. She hadn't finished her Christmas shopping and was still keeping a secret from her family and friends that could destroy long-time relationships. Some people she knew might not be able to handle a white girl pregnant by a black boy. She wondered who would have the nerve to speak honestly, and who would just talk behind her back then she thought of a familiar Bible verse. "Yea, mine own familiar friend, in whom I trusted, which did eat of my bread, hath lifted up his heel against me." (Psalm 41:9)

The road ahead would be difficult for her daughter and grandchild, and her own life would change greatly. She thought of the next verse that gave her comfort for what lay ahead. "But thou, O Lord, be merciful unto me, and raise me up, that I may requite them."

Melanie checked the answering machine. It was blinking. Probably some sales person wanting to sell her a hundred light bulbs for $39.95. She played the message.

"Melanie, this is Ron. I wanted to see if you would have dinner with me Saturday night. Call me, at 233-5901, when you get in."

Melanie smiled. She planned to go, no hesitation whatsoever. She picked up the phone, called Ron, and accepted the date for the Saturday night. When she hung up, she was happy he had called and actually looked forward to seeing him again. The few times they had seen each other had been wonderful.

That night at dinner, Melanie told Morgan not to plan anything for Friday night because she was cooking supper for her and Kevin. She would call Kevin and ask him to come over. She tried to eat with both of them together at least one night a week. It was sort of a bonding night for her and her kids. She liked spending time with just the three of them. Kevin's behavior was getting worse, and she feared what lay ahead. His temper was a lot worse, and she was the last one that he had shown that side to. Recently, he had gotten mad with her about something minor and cursed at her, something he had never done before. Even though Melanie knew it was his brain injury, it hurt her feelings deeply, and it was all she could do to keep from crying in front of him. Seconds after his explosion, he apologized. It broke her heart. He couldn't help himself. It really was beyond his control.

Morgan was wearing a loose-fitting shirt when she came downstairs. She was beginning to show her pregnancy a little. Always before, her clothes had reflected a near-perfect figure. She was a pretty girl with a pretty shape. She was 5'10" and had long blonde hair. Most men looked twice when meeting her on the street. Some looked more than twice. People always said that Morgan could easily have been a model. Some friends had even tried to get her to encourage her daughter to look into a modeling career. Morgan had the looks, but Melanie wasn't sure she had the confidence. She had Melanie's low self-esteem.

They would not be able to hide the truth much longer, but Morgan wanted to wait until after Christmas to tell family she was expecting a baby and that the father was black. Never in their family's history had this happened. There was a first time for everything, but why did her daughter have to be first? Why couldn't someone else's child bring the new millennium into a family that still lived like the Waltons? Her father was eighty-three years old, and her mother was seventy-eight. How would they feel about their first great-grandchild being half-black? Only time would answer that question.

Chapter Seven

$\mathcal{M}$elanie went to work happier on Wednesday than she was the first part of the week. She had a date Saturday night and felt good about it. She peeped into Scarlet's room as she passed and saw Scarlet sitting in a rocking chair looking at a photo album. She knocked on the open door and walked over when Scarlet said, "Come in."

Melanie leaned over and gave Scarlet a tight hug. "Good morning. I hope you are feeling a little better today."

Scarlet shrugged. "Not really," she said sadly. "I want my rings back. I miss the presence of my son in them. They were all I had left of the past and all that I meant to him and him to me. Who would take them from me? Why?"

Melanie shook her head. "I don't know, Scarlet, but we will do everything we can to find them and return them to you. I promise."

That was twice Melanie had promised Scarlet she would find the rings, but she didn't have a clue where to start looking. She didn't like to think anyone could be that low, but she would do all she could to make her promise come true. She wanted to make Scarlet smile again and return that small portion of her son. The woman deserved something to hold on to. No one had the right to take that from her. Melanie hugged Scarlet again and left her alone with her photos and memories.

Melanie went to the kitchenette to fix herself a cup of coffee. Jason was on the couch watching the TV in the sitting area. He looked solemn, as if he didn't have a friend in the world. What a nice looking young man he was. He should be out there enjoying life, being in love, thinking of his future, starting a family—all the things a young man his age usually did. Instead, he was locked up in a psychiatric hospital. Why? What was his big dark secret? She made her coffee, went over to the sofa, and sat down.

"Good morning, Jason."

"Morning," he replied.

"Did you sleep okay last night?" she asked, trying to make conversation.

"No," he replied, not bothering to make eye contact.

"Well, it's hard to sleep in a new environment sometimes," she assured, trying to bond, but not being very successful.

He remained cool and distant.

"Well, guess I better get to work before they kick me out," she said.

"Guess so," Jason agreed.

Melanie stood and turned to walk away, but then turned back. "Jason, I have a son your age. If you ever need to talk, my door is always open."

"Uh-huh," he answered nonchalantly.

She walked to her office feeling as if she had not gotten one bit closer to this boy that she so desperately wanted to help. Melanie was eager for the day to be over, and it had only just begun. Her daydreams about Ron were beginning to scare her a little. It had been a long time since she had met someone so gentlemanly. His manners and thoughtfulness really impressed her. He opened the door for her, helped her with her coat, and walked behind or beside her, never in front of her. His mama had raised him to be an old-fashioned gentleman. He had told her he enjoyed doing those things for a woman and preferred women that allowed men to do such things. It was hard for her to get used to. Often, she would take hold of the door to open it and quickly slip her hand back down and wait for him to open it for her. She was beginning to like being treated like a lady. It was a real change, and it was taking a while for her to get used to it, but she definitely liked it.

Leona stepped through her door, jarring her thoughts back to the present. "We have a team meeting with Jason this morning at 9:30. Try to attend if you can."

"I'll be there. Wouldn't miss it for the world," Melanie teased.

"Yeah, right," nodded Leona.

"Let's hope it's a little more informative than the last two sessions we've had. He's as cold as an iceberg, and we don't seem to be doing a very good job of melting him down."

"I just wish he'd let us help him," replied Melanie.

"Me, too. We can't do it all by ourselves. Maybe somewhere there's a crack in that ice, and we can peck away at it. We just have to keep trying."

"And we will do our very best. If anybody can reach him, Dr. Williams can," Melanie said confidently.

"You're right," Leona agreed.

"Both of us have sons his age, and I think that makes us emotionally involved with this guy. It's such a waste," Melanie said.

Leona nodded. "Yes, it is."

The phone rang. Melanie turned to answer, and Leona left for her office to review Jason's history, what little bit she had. He had not given much information, and he wanted to keep everything to himself. He had a big problem with drugs and alcohol and had been arrested three times for minor offenses—public drunkenness, using obscene language in a local convenience store parking lot, stealing beer from a local fast food store, and driving off without paying for his gas. He was on the road to destruction if he did not get some help soon.

Melanie talked to Dr. Williams on the phone about another new admission coming in. A young black girl from a nearby county would be arriving around one p.m. She was also pregnant. Melanie shuddered at the word, as if an electrical shock had run through her body. Pregnant, pregnant, pregnant. It echoed. Morgan was already beginning to show, and they wouldn't be able to hide the truth much longer. Just give me until after the holidays, she thought. No need to ruin everybody's Christmas.

Melanie told him they would be ready for the girl when she got there. Her family would be bringing her in. Melanie was glad when family was supportive. It was always a big help, and those cases usually had successful endings, but people like Jason had a much harder time.

At 9:15, the care team began to gather in the conference room. Melanie picked up a cup of coffee on the way. If this were not so formal, maybe Jason would relax a little and open up. The doctor was a little intimidating in his white lab coat and bowtie. Dr. Williams was famous for his bowties. Plus, there were three other people in the room making up the care team—all strangers to Jason, trying to pry into his mind. She couldn't help but feel sorry for him.

Jerry brought Jason into the room and they sat down at the table. Jerry was a big guy, at least 6'6", and probably a good 275 pounds. Male nurses were in big demand, and Eastside was fortunate to have him. He could handle most of the behavioral problems single-handedly, if need be, but for the most part, he was a gentle giant.

Jason looked around quickly and then back down at his hands on the table.

"Jason," Dr. Williams started. "Do you know where you are?"

"Yes."

"Tell me where."

"The psychiatric hospital," answered Jason, never looking up.

"Do you know why you're here?"

"Yes."

"Why?"

"Because I was arrested for being drunk in public."

"That's part of it, Jason, but it's more serious than that. You have a drug and alcohol addiction, and you need help. You also have a problem with severe depression. Were you aware of that, Jason?"

"Not really."

"Between the drugs, alcohol, and depression, the judge thought you should spend time here, rather than a jail cell somewhere. He obviously felt there was help for you, or he wouldn't have sent you here. He could just as easily have sent you to prison. We are going to do our best to help you, but you have to want to help yourself."

Jason did not reply. He fiddled with his hands, as if answering the doctor's question might force him to go along with his fate. Dr. Williams never flinched at Jason's disregard for his questions.

"We will start you on medication; you will be going through withdrawal from the drugs and alcohol. Also, you will be on an antidepressant. We also feel you need counseling once a day for the next twenty-one days. Leona will be doing part of your counseling, and we will meet once a week, on Mondays, for discussion. Jason, is there anything you would like to add?"

Jason said nothing. Again, he did not look up.

"Well, I guess that means he agrees with us, team." Dr. Williams knew it meant everything but that, but he smiled, picked up his briefcase, and headed out the door. "See you soon, Jason. Have a good day."

Jerry motioned for Jason to stand, walked with him back to the sitting area, and left him in front of the TV. "Hey, for what it's worth, I've been close to where you are, and it can change for you if you want it to. Give these people a chance, man; they really do care." Jerry patted Jason on the shoulder then turned and walked away, leaving Jason in his own little world, a world made out of stone that no one could enter.

Jason did look up as Jerry walked away, but he made no comment. He had no expression on his face, as he turned back towards the TV.

At lunch, Melanie ran home for a few minutes. She checked the answering machine. No messages. She fixed herself a sandwich and paid some bills while she had a minute. She went by the post office on her way back to the office and dropped off the mail. She saw a lot of people mailing Christmas packages to loved ones. Did anybody wonder where Jason was? Didn't somebody somewhere miss him? Where were his relatives? Surely they would want to know where he was.

Her mind turned to Kevin. If only he could be the way he was before the accident. He loved Christmas so much. He loved playing in the snow with Morgan. One of her favorite pictures was taken in their front yard with Morgan sitting on his shoulders next to a huge snowman they'd built together. He loved to kid around and joke with them. Now he didn't know how to joke. It was like that part of his brain couldn't relate. He very seldom laughed, and when he did, it was a fake laugh because other people were laughing, but she could tell he didn't understand. It was sad to think about the way he used to be and the way he was now. She felt guilty for wishing he was like he had been before the accident. He had come so close to dying that she should be thanking God that he was here, even with a brain injury. She was thankful for his life, but the selfish side of her wanted her son back, the son that loved life, the son that life loved. She remembered his smile and his dimples. Tears filled her eyes.

"Oh, God. I love him so much," she whispered. "Thank you for sparing his life and giving me the opportunity to love him just as he is." Still, in her heart, she yearned for her son back the way he used to be. She missed him so much.

She hurried back to work to admit the young pregnant girl. Tawanna definitely had an attitude with her parents. She must have said the "F" word twenty times during the admission process. Melanie wanted to stuff a rag in her mouth. The girl's problems ran deeper than foul language or she wouldn't be there, so she tried to refrain from being offended. The girl had severe problems to be in a psychiatric hospital. On top of that, she was fifteen years old and pregnant. That alone would give most people an attitude. Melanie's compassion began to resurface. She smiled at the young girl and took hold of her hand.

"Don't be afraid; we are here to help you."

Tawanna bit her bottom lip, and tears rolled down her face. There was a vulnerable side to her, regardless of the tough character she tried to portray.

Leona came to get her to show her to her room. She put her arm around the girl's shoulder, and they walked out of the room. Her parents stayed to give a little more information on their daughter. The father was agitated and not totally happy with leaving his daughter at the hospital. The mother insisted. The father argued with her as they left the hospital.

Melanie wondered why the father would object to his daughter getting treatment. Sometimes it embarrassed a family when kids had to be admitted for psychological treatment. That was probably it. The father was a prominent businessman in town. He worked with a large bank and was very active in church. She had seen his picture in the paper several times after winning awards for some committee he belonged to. Surely he would come to realize it was better she be treated now, especially with a baby on the way. Judging by the looks of her, the birth was not too far away.

Melanie left work depressed. It was always one heartbreak after another. Life was full of challenges.

Morgan was already home when Melanie drove into the driveway, but she hadn't bothered to turn on the house lights. Melanie went upstairs to see if Morgan was in her room. There she was, asleep on her bed. Melanie looked at her, and tears filled her eyes. Did she even know what she was about to face in giving birth to a biracial child in a little southern town? People tried to pretend they were not prejudiced, but they were. "We can work together, but don't come to my house for dinner. My neighbors might see you. Oh, I'm not prejudiced, but my neighbor is." Yada, yada, yada.

Melanie wiped the tears and kissed Morgan lightly on the head. Morgan never even stirred as Melanie tiptoed to the chair and reached for an afghan Grandma had made for her when she was little. Melanie laid it gently over Morgan and stopped again to look at her beautiful daughter. She was innocent, without a clue as to what lay ahead. Melanie gave her credit for one thing. Morgan was determined to protect her unborn child. Melanie knew Morgan loved the baby by the way she talked about it.

Melanie tiptoed from the room, closing the door behind her. She wiped away the tears as she headed back downstairs. She would soon have to tell Morgan's father and the rest of the family. It was not going to be easy. She had promised to wait until after Christmas. Melanie wondered if the KKK still burnt crosses in people's yards. She remembered it happening to a neighbor when she was a child. It had sounded horrible even then. It had frightened her when her mother told her about it, and she had never forgotten it.

Melanie went to her bedroom and flopped down on the bed. She kicked her shoes off and lay back, looking up at the ceiling. She closed her eyes and tried to reassure herself that God would lead the way. She said a little prayer, asking that he show her the way.

"Please give me the strength and the knowledge to do the right thing to help my daughter," she prayed. She asked for guidance and thanked God for his blessings, including her un-born grandchild. She prayed her grandchild would not be caught between two worlds, but welcomed by both. In the per-fect world, he would be accepted equally by both races, but she knew this was far from a perfect world and feared the child may have to pay for the acts of others.

Melanie drifted off to sleep and dreamed. In her dream, there was a baby crying. She kept looking for the baby, but she couldn't find it. It just kept crying, a sad cry, and she couldn't find it. She wanted to comfort it and make it stop crying, but she just couldn't find it. Finally, she woke up, frustrated and exhausted. She had slept for about thirty minutes. It seemed like hours. For some reason, the dream bothered her. Why couldn't she find the baby? And that haunting cry… She shrugged, try-ing to make the memories disappear.

Melanie went to the kitchen to start dinner. Shortly after, Morgan came in to help. They were silent as they worked. Melanie was cooking spaghetti and Morgan was fixing a salad. After a period of silence, Morgan spoke. "I felt the baby move today."

Melanie knew this was the time a grandmother should be ecstatic with joy, but truthfully, she didn't know how to feel. Was she supposed to be happy new life was about to brought into this world—her grandchild? Or sad that the mother was unwed (not exactly the way God preferred it) and the baby bira-cial? She wasn't sure how God felt about the biracial part because truthfully, she had never thought about it before. She knew some people felt races shouldn't mix and felt it was a sin, but Melanie had never read the Bible, so she didn't know the answer. For a moment, Melanie didn't say anything, then, real-izing how awful that looked, Melanie acted happy for her.

"That's good." In her heart, she already loved her grand-child, but she would have preferred a marriage first and a family second, no matter the race. Yes, race did matter to her. White would have been much easier on all of them, including the child. "When do you plan on telling your Daddy?"

"I told you. After Christmas."

"You are already showing a little."

"I can hide it until after Christmas."

They sat down to eat, silent again. Morgan finished eating and went back up to her room. As Melanie finished loading the dishwasher, the phone rang.

"Hello, beautiful."

It was Ron, her shining star. Her spirits lifted instantly.

"What is my lady up to tonight?" He was so sweet she couldn't help but like him.

"We just finished dinner, and I was about to retire with a book for the evening," she answered.

"Well, what if I pick you up and we go for coffee and dessert somewhere, since you have already had dinner."

"Sounds like a great idea. Give me thirty minutes, and I'll be ready."

"It's a date. I'll see you in thirty." He sounded pleased.

Melanie smiled as she jumped into the shower. Yes, this is just what she needed. Ron was good for her and good to her. He was probably the nicest man she had ever met, and she was falling in love with him. She hoped he felt the same about her.

When he arrived, Melanie was just finishing up. She dashed a little perfume on and went downstairs to open the door. Morgan had heard the door bell and answered the door before she got there. Ron was talking to her about her work, and they seemed to hit it off pretty well. Melanie was pleased. She wanted them to like each other. Morgan thought some of the guys she dated were dorks and didn't hesitate to say so. Of course, it worked vise versa, because some of the guys Morgan dated she didn't like, either. She hadn't ever met the father of her grandchild, so she didn't know if she liked him or not. Oh, well, she wasn't about to dwell on that now. She wanted to enjoy the rest of the night.

They went to a small restaurant nearby that was known for their great homemade desserts. Each ordered pie and coffee.

She loved talking with Ron. They had so much in common. They talked about the past and then they talked about what each wanted in the future. Melanie said she did not want to grow old alone and was sorry she would never see a fiftieth wedding anniversary. She envied people like her parents that had been married a long time, and felt she'd lost something by not having that.

She wondered if she'd said too much. She didn't want to scare him off by making him think she was looking for someone to marry. She was not looking for someone to marry but she did want someone to love and someone to love her. She wanted to grow old with somebody she loved. She was afraid of being alone and not having anyone special ever again in her life.

They talked for two hours. Time slipped away in a hurry. Melanie had enjoyed the evening, and she felt Ron had enjoyed it as well. He walked her to the door and smiled down at her.

"I had a great time," he said, smiling.

"I had a great time, also," she said, looking into his blue eyes. Her eyes smiled back at him.

"Do we still have a date Saturday night?" Ron asked.

"I'd be very disappointed if we didn't," she said, still smiling up at him.

He bent down and kissed her lightly on the lips. " I'll call you tomorrow."

"I'll be waiting," she teased.

He laughed as he turned and walked away.

She watched for a moment and then closed the front door and sighed. Yes, she thought, he could be the one she had been praying for. She hoped he was. She was beginning to think there was no one out there for her. She peeped in on Morgan. Fast asleep. Being pregnant had sure changed her night life. A girl her age was not usually home in bed asleep at ten p.m.

Melanie undressed, washed her face, brushed her teeth, and slid into bed. She said her prayers and then spent the next few minutes reliving the evening until she drifted off to sleep.

Chapter Eight

It was five days before Christmas, and Melanie and others at Eastside Hospital were planning a party for the patients. Scarlet had been depressed since the theft of her rings, and Jason was no closer to warming up to them. They had tried all kinds of therapeutic group sessions and one-on-ones, and he still kept his secrets buried. He was distant and rude to everyone. Scarlet was the only one he had not insulted or acted mean to. He ignored her when she talked to him, but he was never rude to her.

Scarlet talked to him like a mother. "Now, you better put your coat on when you go outside to smoke, or you'll catch pneumonia. Pneumonia will kill you, whether you know it or not. My Uncle Jesse had pneumonia when he was forty-two years old and died from it."

She'd hand him his coat, and he'd put it on without even acknowledging her. She kept right on talking to him until he walked out the door to the courtyard where patients went to smoke.

"I declare, you'd think he'd know better. He's twenty-two years old and I still have to tell him to put his coat on when he goes outside. You would think he was nine." She would just go on and on, shaking her head now and then, fussing over him as if he was her child.

Today, the psychiatrist was trying something different with Jason—hypnosis. Rarely was that done here, but when patients refused to open up and discuss their problems, the doctors sometimes turned to more drastic measures. This was one of those cases.

Scarlet was being treated for manic depressive disorder. Some days she talked and talked; other days she stayed to herself. She seemed to be getting better, and Melanie knew it wouldn't be long before the doctors released her. Melanie would miss her. She felt almost like family. She was so warm and friendly you couldn't help but become attached to her.

Melanie wished she could have found out who stole Scarlet's rings. She would love to give her keepsakes back since they were such a valuable memory of her son. Nothing could replace them, ever. The staff had searched every room and every patient, but could not find the rings. Even staff members had been questioned, but nothing had turned up any leads.

Dr. Williams came in, his usual happy self. He had a Christmas bow tie on and was flirting with all the women—or maybe the women were flirting with him. It was hard to tell. Melanie really liked Dr. Williams and had always respected him as a doctor. She trusted him professionally, and whatever he said, she took it next to God's word. He was the one that had suggested hypnosis on Jason. He would do the hypnosis himself there at the hospital today. Leona would assist him, and Melanie had been asked to sit in to take medical notes. She had mixed feelings about being present when someone revealed things they may not want others to know. Obviously, Jason did not want to share his feelings, or he would have already done it.

Jerry was asked to go get Jason as Leona and Dr. Williams discussed the procedure. Leona had done this before with Dr. Williams. This was Melanie's first time being present for a hypnosis session, and she was a little nervous.

Jason stepped into the room and looked around. "What's going on?"

"We are going to do hypnosis, Jason. We believe it may help you."

"On me? No!" Jason answered.

"Jason, you can try to help yourself here, or you can go to Cherry Hospital for long-term treatment. It's up to you. I don't believe you want to spend the rest of your life in a mental hospital, but it's up to you."

Dr. Williams was firm and direct. He always told it just like it was—good, bad, or ugly. He didn't play around when it came to his patients.

Jason was silent for a moment. "It won't do any good."

"Well, it won't do any good if we don't do it, either, will it?" Dr. Williams asked. He sat on the edge of his chair with his elbows on his knees and his face resting on his fist as he stared at Jason. "All I'm asking for, son, is a chance to help you. That's all."

Jason looked into Dr. Williams' eyes. For a moment, neither said a word. Dr. Williams just stared back, waiting for an answer.

"Okay," Jason said, throwing up his hands. "Whatever."

Dr. Williams slapped Jason on the knee. "Okay, then. Let's do it."

Leona dimmed the lights. Melanie could barely see her notepad. Even though Dr. Williams had a recorder on, he wanted Melanie to note Jason's behavior—things a recording couldn't show—like facial expressions and body language. Dr. Williams told Jason to close his eyes and count slowly backwards, starting at one hundred. He told him to relax and picture himself as a child, outside, by the lake near his house, throwing stones into the water. He was teaching Billy to skip stones across the water, and it was a warm day.

"Think about your childhood, Jason; go back to the day your daddy died. You're twelve years old; tell me what you see. Jason sat quietly for a moment, as if drifting back in time.

"I see my daddy," he said suddenly, his voice changing, becoming higher-pitched and uncertain. "He's walking up the path. Oh, no. He's drunk again. My little brother runs and hides. He's afraid Daddy'll hit him again. I'm not going to run and hide. I'm twelve years old. Twelve–year-olds aren't afraid of their daddies."

Silence.

"Go on, Jason. What else do you see?" Dr. Williams coaxed.

"He comes over to where I'm throwing stones in the lake. I try to ignore him. He's cursing at me. 'You are a damn no-good kid,'" snarls Jason, his voice now harsh, slurred, and angry. 'Why didn't you cut the grass like I told you to?'" His voice changes again. "'The lawn mower is broke, Daddy, and I couldn't get it started.'"

Jason's face twists. "'I'm going to beat your God damn ass.'" Then he jumps and dodges an invisible blow. "He swings at me. I jump around, trying to get away, but he grabs me and throws me to the ground and kicks me in the side. 'You are a lazy-ass boy, and I wish you'd never been born. Your sorry Mama ain't no better than you are. She's a no-good bitch.'"

Silence.

"Jason, go on. What else do you see?"

"My mama."

"What about your mama?"

"She's watching from the kitchen window. She's crying. He kicks me again. I can't get up. It hurts so bad. I don't want to cry. I don't want him to see me cry. He'll keep kicking me until I cry. He pulls me up by my hair and slaps me in the face. 'What are you laughing at, boy?'"

"I'm not laughing, Daddy. 'What did you say, boy?' I'm not laughing. He slaps me again and my lip is bleeding. I start to cry."

Silence. Jason has tears in his eyes and suddenly, he's fully there, back in the past, reliving the nightmare.

"Daddy, please don't hit me again.

"'You are a crying-ass baby. You never have been worth a damn. I just might lock you in the barn all night to toughen you up. Come here, you sorry-ass. I'm going to lock you up in the barn.'

"Please, Daddy, don't do that. I'll be good, I promise.

"'You've never been good in your life. You and your brother ain't worth a damn! Where is your brother? I got something for him, too.'

"Daddy, he's only five years old. Leave him alone!

"'I'll find him. I know where he hides.'

"Daddy, stop. Don't hurt him.

"'Get out of my way! You sorry ass.'

Jason starts to sob. Melanie wants to comfort him and looks at the doctor. Dr. Williams puts up his hand for everyone to stay still. In a few moments, he continues, wiping his face with both hands.

"Daddy goes into the house to look for Billy. I'm pulling on his coat, and he slaps me again across the face. My face is bleeding pretty bad now, and my side hurts when I move. I'm still crying, begging him not to hurt Billy. I hear Billy crying under his bed. Daddy staggers to the bedroom, looks under the bed, and starts to laugh.

"You thought you could hide from me you little weasel?" Jason screams, his father's words pouring from his mouth. Then he's himself again, huddled in a ball in his chair like a frightened child.

"He pulls Billy out by the hair. Billy is crying and scared. I'm still pulling at his coat begging him not to hurt Billy. Daddy, please, he's little! He hasn't done anything! Daddy, stop! He smacks Billy in the face and his head snaps backwards. Billy is fighting back, screaming, 'Daddy, stop! Daddy, you're hurtin' me!'

"I'm begging him to stop. I'm trying to get between him and Billy. He pushes me hard, and I fall on the floor. Billy is hollering and kicking. Daddy smacks him again in the face, harder this time, and his head snaps backwards again. I hear a pop, and Billy stops kicking. His body goes limp and his little head falls back. Daddy, stop! You've hurt him really bad! I'm pulling on Daddy's arm, blood is dripping from my lip and nose, and my side hurts, but I have to help Billy. He is so little, and I am his big brother. It's up to me to help him.

"'He's as sorry as you are. Neither of you should have ever been born.'" Jason's voice turns ugly again, and his words slur.

Then he's himself, scared and small and trembling with the memories. "He throws Billy down on his bed." Jason starts to cry again, putting his head in his hands and weeping.

Melanie wiped her eyes. The tears dropped onto her notepad, making the words run together. She felt like weeping right along with Jason. Her heart went out to him. They all sat silent, waiting for Jason to continue.

After a few moments, Dr. Williams spoke softly. "Jason, go on. What happened next?"

"Daddy staggers out of the bedroom. He's swearing about me and Billy being no good. I run to Billy, but he's not moving. He's not crying, either. I wonder why he's not crying. I pick

him up and his head falls backwards. Billy, wake up! Wake up!
Say something! Wake up! Please, Billy, wake up!

"He feels like a rag doll in my arms. I can't wake him up. I
start to cry and hug him close to me. Billy, please, if you love
me, wake up! I need you!

"He still doesn't move. His eye is swollen and there're cuts
on his face. He isn't going to wake up. He'll never wake up
again. My daddy broke his neck. I hug Billy close for a few
minutes and lay him on his bed. I feel like I let him down. He's
only five years old. He didn't deserve this. I stare at Billy for a
few minutes, and I know what I have to do.

"Mama comes into Billy's room and sees him on the bed.
She knows he's dead as soon as she sees him. She screams, falls
to her knees beside his bed, and pulls him into her arms. She's
crying hysterically and rocks him in her arms. 'Oh, my poor
baby. My poor baby. My poor baby. I love you, Billy. Mama
loves you. Mama loves you, baby. Mama's sorry, baby. Mama's
sorry. I love you so much, baby. Mama's sorry, baby.' She's
sitting on the floor, rocking him, holding his head to her chest.

"Mama gets up, still holding Billy in her arms, and his head
falls back across her arm. She pulls him closer, resting his head
on her chest, and then she kisses him. She is still crying, telling
Billy she is sorry and loves him. She walks into the kitchen
where Daddy is sitting at the kitchen table with a pint of whis-
key. He takes a swallow from the bottle. 'You killed him! You
killed my baby!' Tears stream down her face.

"'He ain't dead, bitch.'

"'You killed my baby! You killed my baby! You bastard!'
She kicks him as hard as she can on the leg.

"Daddy comes out of the chair and starts at her, his hand up
in the air, ready to hit her."

"BAM!" Jason suddenly jerked back as if firing a rifle, his
eyes wide open. Melanie almost jumped out of her chair, and
then she froze. They were all frozen. It was like watching a hor-
ror movie, only worse, because they were actually living the
movie. Jason was frozen, too. He didn't move for a few minutes. He just stared, as if he couldn't believe it himself. Then he

suddenly relaxed and started to weep again. Tears ran down his face.

"That's for Billy, Daddy!" Jason buried his face in his hands and wept.

Dr. Williams waited a few minutes and wiped his own eyes. He spoke softly, and his voice showed his emotion. "Jason, go on."

"When the police arrive, my mama tells them she shot my daddy in self-defense. No one ever knew I killed him. Mama never told a soul, and neither did I. After the funeral, we moved away. Six years later, my Mom died of breast cancer." Jason wiped his eyes and nose.

Dr. Williams spoke softly. "Jason, look by the lake. There is a rose bush. It has beautiful red roses on it. Do you see it?"

Silence.

"Yes, I see it."

"Go to the rose bush and pick three of the prettiest roses you see."

"Okay, I have three red roses in my hand."

"Now, Jason, look just beyond the rose bush, and you will see your daddy, your mama, and your brother. They are waiting for you. Take the first red rose and give it to your daddy. Tell him you forgive him for killing Billy."

Jason lifted his hand in the air. "Daddy, I forgive you for killing Billy."

"Now ask your daddy to forgive you."

"Daddy, please forgive me for what I did to you." His lips trembled.

"Give him a hug and say goodbye."

Jason circled his arms, hugging the air. "Goodbye, Daddy." Jason wiped his cheek.

"Now, Jason, take the second rose and give it to your little brother. Tell him you love him."

Again, Jason held up his hand. He handed the rose to his brother. "Here, Billy. I'm sorry I couldn't save you. I tried, I really did, but he was so big and so strong. I miss you and I love you," Jason said softly, his voice quivering.

"Now hug him and tell him goodbye."

"Goodbye, Billy." He leaned over, as if embracing his little brother.

"I'll never forget you, Billy Goat." Jason smiled at the nickname. He hugged Billy goodbye then put his hand out and waved it around, as if tussling Billy's hair. Again his face saddened and he wiped the tears away.

"The third rose is for your mama," Dr. Williams said gently. "Give the third rose to your mama. Give her a hug and tell her you love her."

Jason kissed the imaginary rose gently. Tears streamed down his face. "Here, Mama. This rose is for you."

Melanie put her hand over her mouth, trying not to sob out loud. Her heart was breaking for Jason.

"Jason, tell your mama goodbye," Dr. Williams coaxed.

Jason looked like a child that had lost everything he loved. "Mama, I love you so much," he said sadly.

For a moment, he lingered with his hand in the air, as if not wanting to turn loose of the rose—or the memory of his mother. Slowly, he began to smile. The look on his face was hard to describe. Contentment. Something none of them had seen since meeting him.

Finally, he appeared to let go of the rose, and he again embraced the empty air as if it were his beloved mama. He lingered a few moments, taking in the imaginary embrace, his eyes closed, and then slowly, he backed away. "Goodbye, Mama. I know you are happy in Heaven with Billy." He smiled again. "I know you're watching over me, I feel your presence sometimes. Don't worry about me, Mama. I will see you and Billy again one day." He wiped the tears from his cheeks.

Jason turned away, leaving his mama behind in Heaven to take care of Billy.

"Now, Jason," Dr. Williams whispered hoarsely. "There is a mirror to the left of you. Go stand in front of the mirror."

Jason turned slightly to the left.

"Look into the mirror. Tell the person in the mirror that you love him and forgive him."

"The person in the mirror is me," Jason said, a little surprised.

"That's correct," Dr. Williams answered.

Jason's lips trembled, and tears slowly spilled onto his cheeks again. "I love you, Jason, and I forgive you." His voice cracked, and his head dropped. He began to cry again, softly this time. He put his elbows on his knees and his face in his hands.

Melanie wiped the tears from her face and so did Leona. They were all silent.

"Jason," Dr. Williams said after a few moments. "Start to count backwards from one hundred, and open your eyes when you are ready."

After a few seconds, Jason opened his eyes. He seemed surprised to find his face was wet. He wiped his face with the back of his hand, as if trying to hide his emotions. "Why is my face wet?" Jason asked, curious.

"You said goodbye to your family," Dr. Williams answered softly.

"Well, if I was able to do that, I believe in miracles," Jason said as he stood.

"Well, son, I do believe in miracles," Dr. Williams answered. "I have witnessed a few miracles in my lifetime."

"Thanks, Dr. Williams, for trying to help," Jason said. He stuck out his hand to shake Dr. William's hand.

Melanie was shocked.

"You're welcome, son." Dr. Williams took hold of Jason's hand and then hugged him.

Jason left the conference room, went to his room, and shut the door. Dr. Williams sighed. He looked tired and said nothing as he went into his office and shut the door behind him.

Melanie was impressed. She sat in the room, exhausted, as if she had just lived the last ten years of Jason's life. It was not a pleasant feeling. No one knew if the session had helped. Time would tell. It had to help just saying goodbye to his family and forgiving his daddy and himself. That's why he didn't have any support; they were all dead. The shocking truth was that Jason had killed his daddy, not his mother as the police report had said. Poor Jason, she thought. What a tragic life. Melanie couldn't imagine what she would do without her family for support. She sat for a moment, lost in thought. A tear ran down her face, and she quickly wiped it away.

Slowly, she pushed her chair back, stood, walked to the window, and stared into the street. Below, people went about their normal routines. No one knew what was going on in their lives. She watched two young boys throwing a football and wondered what their home lives were like. Were they victims of an abusive mother or father? Would they turn out like Jason? She hoped they would be spared the agony of such a curse. Her eyes burned from holding back more tears.

"Get a grip," she told herself. "You are a professional. Don't get emotionally involved."

Finally, she gave up and let the tears roll down her face. She had so much of her own to bear, and now she felt like she was bearing Jason's tragedy, too.

Jason had definitely touched their lives today, and none of them would soon forget the dramatic reliving of Jason's ongoing nightmare, the horrible secret he had been carrying all these years. Melanie hoped Dr. Williams had helped Jason find peace and a new beginning.

Chapter Nine

Melanie left work thinking about all she had to do before Christmas. She thought of Morgan and wondered how they would get through Christmas and keep her pregnancy a secret when she was already beginning to show. It would not be long before the explosion of accusations, disappointment, and retaliations from Morgan's father, family, and friends began.

Melanie had always thought Morgan was a strong person, but she knew the challenge this time would be a lot to bear. She again thought of herself as a grandmother and wondered what the baby should call her. Grandma? Nana? MeMa? She laughed out loud. Grandma? That sounded old to her. She would have to think about that some more.

Ron called on her cell phone. "Hi, sweetie!"

"Hello," she said with a smile in her voice.

"Just calling to see if you wanted to go get pizza tonight."

"Sure, but is it okay if Morgan comes with us? I really don't want to make her eat alone again tonight."

"Of course. That would be great," he said, sounding glad Morgan was going with them.

"How about if Morgan and I meet you there?" she said.

"No problem. Name the time," he said.

"How is six-thirty?" Melanie asked.

"That would be great," Ron replied quickly. "Dinner with two beautiful ladies—how lucky can a man be?" He sounded happy.

Melanie smiled as she hung up the phone, glad she had included Morgan.

Morgan was already home when Melanie popped in the door, suddenly refreshed from her day at the hospital. That phone call from Ron must have given her the sudden burst of energy. Whatever it was, she liked the feeling.

"We are invited out to dinner by a gentleman," Melanie told Morgan in a southern accent.

"Oh, my gracious. What shall I wear?" Morgan answered, falling right into the role of a southern bell.

"Well, my dear, I think your jeans will be fine enough."

"Yes, ma'am. I will wear my finest jeans."

They broke out laughing. It had been a few days since there had been any laughter in this house, and it felt good to lift the atmosphere. Melanie ran upstairs to jump into the shower and put on fresh makeup. She wanted to look her best, just in case he was the knight in shining armor she had been waiting for.

When Morgan came downstairs, she was dressed in jeans and a black, loose-fitting top that really didn't show her pudgy belly. The top was gathered at the bodice, held by a silver clasp, and flowed softly down around her waist. She wore silver dangly earrings and a silver necklace. It was just dressy enough to look nice for dinner, even though she was wearing jeans. Melanie thought Morgan looked very pretty and was proud she was going to dinner with her and Ron. Melanie was wearing jeans and a red scoop-neck sweater that complimented her blonde hair, gold hoop earrings, and a gold locket her mother had given her for Christmas last year. People had told her she looked a lot like Michele Pfeiffer. She couldn't see it, but she appreciated the compliment. Morgan was about a head taller than Melanie, but favored Melanie in her green eyes. She favored Dan around her lips and nose, and the older Kevin got, the more he favored Dan—around his eyes especially.

"You look pretty," Melanie told Morgan.

"You, too," Morgan said.

"Ready?" Melanie asked, smiling.

"Yep. Waiting on you."

Melanie gave Morgan's stomach a little pat. "Is Baby ready?"

"Yep. We're both ready," Morgan answered. "And we're both hungry." She grinned.

"What else is new?" Melanie said, laughing.

"The sooner we get there, the sooner I can eat."

"Try not to eat him out of his whole week's paycheck, please; he may not ask us again."

"I'll try not to, but I can't make any promises for the baby," Morgan giggled.

"No excuses," Melanie said, spanking Morgan on the butt as they went out the door.

Dinner went smoothly, with small talk about work and jobs, the food, the Christmas season, and whatever else popped up. Melanie thought Ron and Morgan hit it off pretty well. She was pleased with the way they warmed up to one another. Finally, she thought, someone that could actually fit into her life. When Ron walked them to her car, Morgan got in and turned on the radio while Melanie stood outside for a moment, telling Ron what a good time she'd had.

Ron bent and kissed her lightly on the cheek. "I'll give you a call tomorrow, if that's okay."

"I'd like that," Melanie replied. She got in her car, light-hearted. For a moment, all her problems seemed to vanish.

Morgan was in her own little world as they drove the four blocks home. Melanie glanced over, but Morgan was looking out the window as if in deep thought. Morgan went to her room when they got home, and Melanie read some of a book she had been trying to read for a month. She thought she should write a book. It would probably be a best seller.

Chapter Ten

*F*riday finally came; there were only four days until Christmas. Everyone at work was in a festive mood, and Christmas music played over the intercom throughout the day, bringing more spirit to those that cared to join in the seasonal fun. Brightly wrapped gifts were under the tree—some for staff and some for residents. Most of the staff gifts were gag gifts left by other staff members. Some family members had brought gifts for their loved ones and left them to be opened on Christmas morning. Melanie placed Leona's gift under the tree and saw a small box wrapped in what appeared to be a paper towel and taped very securely. It had written on it "To Ms. Scarlet." Melanie wondered who would wrap a gift in a paper towel, but figured it was a gag gift from one of the nurses or staff. She smiled, hoping it would lift Scarlet's spirit. She had really been down since the theft of her rings. Scarlet was doing better and her mood swings had pretty much stabilized. She was doing great in group therapy and had been like a mother to some of the other residents. She particularly liked Jason and Tawanna. As hard as she tried with them, they were like rocks, not wanting to socialize with the others. Still, she tried. She would talk to Jason for an hour at a time without so much as acknowledgement from him. She patted him on the head each time she left him and said, "It'll be all right, son; you just hang in there. I'm praying for you, and I feel it in my bones. You are going to be okay."

Tawanna was seven months pregnant. She often secluded herself from the others in the group room by going into a corner with her CD player and headphones. She only talked if spoken to and then as little as possible. She was such a pretty girl. Melanie figured she had a boyfriend somewhere that she was missing. Obviously, she had a boyfriend, or she wouldn't be pregnant.

Tawanna was a light-skinned African-American with pretty brown eyes and black hair. Her family was well liked in the community. Her father was president of Eastside Bank and her grandfather had been a well-known attorney. He had passed away last year of a massive heart attack while in the court room. The newspaper wrote a big article on his accomplishments and contributions to the community. Melanie had always thought he was very distinguished looking and handsome for a man his age and Tawanna obviously favored him.

Dr. Williams was scheduled to meet with Tawanna at eleven a.m. Melanie was to assist Dr. Williams with his one-on-one consultations. Melanie got Tawanna when it was time for her session. Tawanna walked into the room and sat at the table. On her left wrist was a gauze bandage. Melanie had seen this more than once and knew exactly what it meant. Tawanna had attempted suicide. Melanie flipped open the medical chart and glanced down at the history. She was right. She was not surprised, but why would being pregnant cause a young girl to want to end her life? Even if the father didn't want anything to do with the baby, she didn't think that would make her that desperate. Her family would be there for her, wouldn't they? She had a really nice family, and from what she knew about them, she felt they would be very supportive.

Dr. Williams sat down across from Tawanna and took her hand. "Tawanna, I am here to help you. Anything you tell me will be kept confidential."

Tawanna gave Dr. Williams a faint smile. He patted her hand and gave her a fatherly smile. She seemed to relax a little.

"Tawanna when is your baby due?" Dr. Williams asked.

"February 19," she answered shyly.

"And do you want this baby?"

"No, sir, I don't," she answered, without hesitation.

Dr. Williams looked a little surprised by her answer. "And why not?"

"Just because."

"Just because why?" Dr. Williams probed.

Tawanna looked away, her eyes stinging. She just shook her head slowly.

"Tawanna, I want you to look at me," Dr. Williams said.

She slowly turned to look into his inquiring eyes.

"Why?" he asked firmly.

"I just don't want this baby. I want a baby someday, but not this baby." Again, she fought the tears.

Dr. Williams leaned over and touched Tawanna's hand. "Sweetie, you have your whole life ahead of you. This pregnancy is not going to ruin your life. Sure, it will slow it down, but you are a strong young lady, and you can overcome this. You have to believe in yourself. Your family will be there for you."

Tawanna took her hand back and looked away. This time, the tears won. They moved down her pretty face. Melanie got up, got some tissues, and gave them to her.

Tawanna wiped her eyes and face and looked at Dr. Williams. "I'm sorry."

"No need to be sorry, sweetheart. We all have emotions, and sometimes we have to let everything out. Crying helps relieve the pressure we feel inside. Cry all you want."

After thirty minutes of trying to coax her into telling him why she didn't want the baby, he told her to make a list of all the reasons to keep the baby and all the reasons not to keep the baby, and he would discuss it with her in their next meeting. Tawanna nodded and looked away, wiping her tears with the palm of her hands.

Dr. Williams sat there a moment and just looked at her, as if trying to unlock the secret she had buried so deeply. He had seen many unmarried, pregnant young ladies, but it didn't lead them to the point of suicide. Was she afraid of shaming a prominent family name? Not likely. Even though it could cause some embarrassment, he just couldn't make a connection to the burden the girl seemed to be carrying. Why wouldn't she just say what was on her mind?

Tawanna pushed the chair back and stood up. She walked out of the room, sniffling.

Dr. Williams slapped his legs. "Well, girls, that's another day at Eastside. I'm going home to my lovely wife and having a glass of wine and dinner. I want to try to relax a little before it's time to start all over again." Dr. Williams was a compassionate person, and he, too, got emotionally attached to some of his clients. He had let it happen again today with Tawanna. Dr. Williams had a daughter, and maybe that's why he seemed so caught up in Tawanna's case. Melanie, too, was ready to call it a day and go home.

Melanie got home about six o'clock and found Morgan in the kitchen fixing sloppy Joes for supper. Morgan had never been one to volunteer to cook. This was a new and welcome experience.

"What's the occasion?" asked Melanie, surprised.

"No occasion. Just hungry."

"Oh-ho. So now you cook?"

"I was starving, and you weren't here, so the only option was to cook."

"Okay, well, I'm not complaining. In fact, I'm delighted. I've had a rough day, and the help is greatly appreciated."

Morgan's pregnancy was showing more now, and she was eating more now that she was eating for two. She wondered again how Morgan would hide her pregnancy through Christmas. Melanie put plates on the table, poured them each a glass of tea, and found some potato chips to go with the sloppy Joes. They sat down at the kitchen bar and fixed their plates of food.

"Mama, I've been thinking about names. If it's a boy, I want to name him Noah, and if it's a girl, I want to name her Crystal."

Melanie thought for a moment as she chewed her food. "Yeah, I like both those names."

She waited a moment and then said, "What about the last name? Are you going to use the daddy's last name or yours?"

Morgan thought a minute. "Well, we've talked about it, and I told him I would use his last name," she answered, watching her mother's expression.

"Morgan, have you thought about the fact that if you don't marry this man, you and your child will have different last names forever and that whenever someone addresses you, they will call you by the child's last name, assuming the child's last name is the same as yours?" She paused and continued. "Also, other children will wonder why he or she has a different last name than his or her mama. I think you should use your last name. It will be a lot less confusing for everyone, especially the child."

Melanie doubted her opinion would do any good, since Morgan had always done things pretty much her way, no matter what anybody else thought. She figured this would be no different.

"But he wants me to give the baby his last name," Morgan argued.

"What if in a couple of years he backs out of your lives, for whatever reason? Your child would still have his name but no daddy."

"Mama, why do you always have to look on the negative side?" Morgan asked.

"It's not negative, Morgan; it happens all the time. It's called reality," Melanie said.

Morgan sighed. Melanie knew when to stop, and so she did. She had planted a seed for thought, and that was all she could do. Melanie finished her food and got up to go watch her favorite sitcom, *Seinfeld*. Sometimes it made her laugh out loud, and after a day like today, she needed a little comic relief.

Morgan put the dishes in the dishwasher and joined Melanie in the den. It wasn't long before Morgan drifted off to sleep. Melanie remembered how tired and sleepy she was when she was pregnant. Eat and sleep; sleep and eat. Gosh, it didn't seem that long ago, and now here she was about to be a grandma. Melanie watched Morgan as she breathed, so peaceful, as if she didn't have a worry in the world. Melanie loved her child and worried about what lay ahead. If only she could protect her and her baby from all the cruelties, but she knew she could not. All she could do was stand beside her and help her though the difficult times. Melanie eased the recliner back, and she, too, drifted off to sleep.

She awakened about an hour later and decided to go up to bed. She gently shook Morgan and told her she was going to bed. Morgan seemed to think that was a good idea and decided to do the same. Melanie hugged her. I love you."

"I love you, too," Morgan said sleepily.

Melanie checked the doors to make sure they were locked and went to her room. She heard the phone ring and Morgan pick it up in her room. It must be the mystery man. I guess I'll meet him eventually. She climbed into bed and gave in to sleep. She seemed to stay so tired lately. She figured it had to do with being so emotionally drained all the time. Dealing with the emotions at work was bad enough, but now she had to deal with her son's brain injury and keep Morgan's pregnancy secret. It was a lot for one person to bear with no loving arms for support. Maybe that part of her life was about to change. She truly hoped so. She wanted to find her best friend and spend the rest of her life with him. Maybe Ron was that person.

There were only two days before Christmas, and Melanie worried her family would be able to tell that Morgan was pregnant. She was showing a little now. They would soon have to be told, and so would Morgan's father. She wasn't looking forward to that day.

Melanie moved through the grocery store, gathering food for her Christmas Eve dinner. She wanted to invite Ron over. It would give him a chance to bond with Morgan and Kevin. She was actually happy. She guessed the Christmas spirit had finally won her over. While she was at the store, she decided to pick up a few items for a little party at work that the staff was planning for the residents. It had to be a lonely time for them. It could have been worse. At least they had staff and other residents to keep them company. It had to be better than being all alone, like Jason. If it weren't for them, he would be spending Christmas alone. Melanie was not glad he was at Eastside, but she was glad he was not going to be alone. There were probably others there in the same situation.

Melanie rushed, for she still had much to do. The sky was beginning to turn dark, and the weatherman had predicted a white Christmas. That would be nice, but she wanted her family to get home for Christmas safely. Her brother Charles, and his wife Carol, and Joan and her husband Steve and their kids had to travel over a hundred miles to get to her mama and daddy's house, and her mother had spent days preparing the big Christmas meal. She shuddered at the thought of missing Christmas with her family. They had never missed a Christmas together except when Charles was in the army and stationed in Germany. Christmas was like all holidays to her family; it was important to be together.

Last Christmas, it snowed Christmas night, and they were all stranded an extra night. That was okay; they actually enjoyed the extra time together, not to mention being able to eat all that good food an extra day. She felt her parents were glad it had snowed and they all got to stay an extra day. It was just another memory to add to the family scrapbook, a scrapbook limited in time, Melanie thought sadly, thinking about her daddy's declining health.

Melanie's cell phone rang, breaking into her thoughts.

"Hi, gorgeous," Ron said on the other end.

"Hi," she said, smiling.

"I was calling to check on you, to see if there was anything I could bring to dinner on Christmas Eve. A bottle of wine, maybe?"

"Sure. That would be great," she said, laughing.

"And what else?"

"Just yourself and a big appetite." She couldn't stop smiling. What is it?

"Okay, then. I will see you tomorrow night. I am looking forward to it," Ron said.

"Me, too," she said, and she honestly meant it. It would be fun.

She finished shopping and went to work to help prepare for the residents' party. She slipped little gifts under the tree for each resident. She had especially become fond of Scarlet, Jason, and Tawanna. Each had a special place in her heart.

Scarlet saw Melanie and came over to share some conversation about Christmases' past, when her son was a child. When she talked about him, her face lit up and her voice had a happy tone. "I remember when he got his first BB gun. He was nine years old. We told him to be careful," she said, starting to laugh. "First thing he did, he went outside, shot his new BB gun, missed his target board, and shot the neighbor's tail light out of his brand-new Ford pickup truck. His daddy was so embarrassed when he had to go next door and tell the neighbor our son had shot the tail light out on his new truck. Luckily, our neighbor had two sons of his own and understood. After that, his dad moved the target board to face the woods, not the neighbor's driveway.

"Then there was the time he got a go-cart for Christmas," she said, pausing to laugh. "He rode that thing in a bumpy field for so long that he had bruises all down his legs. He looked like he had been beaten." She wiped away the tears from laughing so hard. "Those were the days," she said, her smile slowly fading. Sadness returned as reality took over. "If only," she said. "If only."

Melanie could relate because she had said those same words many times about Kevin. She felt herself sadden, caught herself, and tried to lighten the mood. She grabbed Scarlet and hugged her. "Come on. Help me get the refreshments."

"Okay," said Scarlet, walking with Melanie towards the kitchen arm-in-arm.

Jason came up and stood close as they fixed the table. "Well, Jason, don't just stand there, son. Give me a hand here, please," said Scarlet, mostly just to include him in the activities, Melanie felt.

Jason moved closer and helped Scarlet put the red tablecloth on the table. Scarlet started singing along with the Christmas music playing on the intercom. She had a very nice voice and sang beautifully.

"I used to sing in the church choir when I was young," she said proudly. "That was when I believed there was a God. Now I'm not so sure he's really out there." She pondered for a moment. "If he is out there, I'm mad at him. How could he let so many bad things happen to me? My son, my husband, my best friend—all gone. Why? What did I ever do to deserve losing everyone I loved most?"

Jason just listened, and Melanie thought she saw tears forming in his eyes. Jason looked away, and so did Melanie, so as not to make him uncomfortable. Leona popped in the door with arms full of gifts and food. Melanie went to help her put gifts under the tree. Scarlet and Jason took the food Leona brought and put it on the table.

Tawanna had wandered over, and so had some of the other residents. Everyone was beginning to lighten up a little and enjoy the Christmas togetherness. Even Tawanna had a smile on her pretty face for the first time. Dr. Williams arrived, so it was time to start the festivities. Then Santa arrived. Melanie looked at Leona, but Leona looked as surprised as she did. Both shrugged their shoulders at the same time. They looked at Dr. Williams.

"What?" he grinned. "Can't have Christmas without Santa Claus, can you?"

"Certainly not." Melanie winked at Dr. Williams.

"Bless you, Doc."

Santa came in, went to the Christmas tree, and picked up the first gift. As each name was called, the residents received their gifts—some from staff, some from family, and even one from Santa Claus himself. Residents were busy opening gifts when all of a sudden, a scream ripped through the room, making everyone jump.

"What in the name of God happened?" Melanie asked, jumping to her feet.

Scarlet was crying, holding her hands over her mouth as if trying to muffle the sobs.

"What is it, Scarlet?" Dr. Williams asked rushing to Scarlet.

Scarlet couldn't speak she was sobbing so hard.

"Is she having a heart attack?" Jason asked, concerned.

"I don't think so," replied Dr. Williams, looking at Scarlet closely.

Melanie put her arm around Scarlet's shoulders.

"What's wrong, Scarlet?"

"Please tell us what the matter is. Do you hurt anywhere?" Dr. Williams asked.

Scarlet lifted her face and wiped the tears away. She held up her hands, and at first it didn't register, then the diamond rings came into focus. Melanie felt weak inside. They were the rings her son had made that had been stolen.

Scarlet beamed. "My rings. My beautiful rings that I love so much."

Dr. Williams smiled from ear to ear, and so did the rest of the staff and residents.

"Where did they come from, Scarlet?" asked Dr. Williams.

"They were in a small box wrapped in a paper towel," she said, laughing and crying at the same time. "I don't care where they came from. I am thankful to whoever brought them to me. Thank you, thank you, thank you," she said looking around the room. Scarlet looked upward, "Thank you, God, for answering my prayers." Then Scarlet started to sing softly, "Silent night, holy night. All is calm. All is bright…"

After a few phrases, other residents and staff joined in. For a few moments, it was like everyone was family. It put the true feeling of Christmas in the air.

When she finished singing, Scarlet looked towards heaven and said, "Merry Christmas, son. I love you."

Jason turned and walked away, his head hanging.

The others gathered around, talking, laughing, and hugging, giving Christmas wishes.

After a few moments, Melanie went to Jason's room and knocked softly on the door. Jason was lying on his bed with an arm over his forehead and his eyes closed. Melanie knocked again. She knew he was not asleep. "Jason, can I talk with you?"

"I guess so," he said quietly.

"Jason, why did you leave the party so soon?"

Jason sat up and Melanie pulled a chair closer. "Jason, I just want to know that you are okay."

"I'm fine," he said, looking down and then back at Melanie.

"Jason, I know this time of year is especially hard for you, since you don't have any family," she said kindly.

"I'm used to it," he replied sadly.

"Do you ever get used to not having your family around?" Melanie asked.

"Yeah, you learn not to think about how it could have been or what your life is compared to every one else's, and then things don't seem so bad. Ms. Melanie, I have a confession to make," Jason said, looking Melanie in the eyes.

"What is it, Jason?" she asked, concerned.

Jason hesitated, as if trying to decide whether to go any further. "I was the one that stole Ms. Scarlet's rings."

For some reason, Melanie was not surprised. "Why, Jason?" she asked softly.

"I really don't know. It was like I was jealous that she had a son that was so special to her and that she was so proud of." Jason looked down. "I felt bad after I did it. I didn't even think how bad it would hurt her. I really didn't like seeing her cry."

"Jason, you should tell Scarlet and apologize to her," she told him.

"I can't face her," he said.

"Jason, she will understand. She likes you a lot."

"Well, she won't like me when she finds out I was the one that took her rings," he said.

"I feel sure she will forgive you, Jason. She is a very compassionate person, and I know for a fact that she thinks the world of you."

"I don't know," he said.

"Jason, you have to tell her."

"Maybe later," he said.

"Whenever you feel up to it," Melanie said, putting her hand on his arm.

"Okay, I will."

"Now, do you want to come back and join the party?" she asked hopefully.

Jason lay back down. "No, I think I will just stay here and rest."

"All right. If that's what you want to do—but we really do wish you would join us," she said, trying to convince him to join the Christmas festivities.

"Thanks for asking," he said, "but I'd rather be alone."

"Sure. Just remember we all care about you," she said, leaning closer and patting his arm.

Melanie stood and moved the chair back. "Goodnight, Jason."

"Goodnight."

Melanie returned to the party. Several residents had gone to their rooms to be alone, but others enjoyed the company. Scarlet was still talking and laughing with anyone that would talk to her. She definitely was happy. Melanie was thankful for that.

After the party, Melanie and Leona put the leftovers away, and Scarlet came over to help.

"God bless the soul that returned my rings," she said happily. "Today was almost as happy as the first time I saw them. Bryan gave me the first one on Mother's day. He was so secretive about the whole thing. He took one of my other rings and said he was going to clean it, when he really was getting the size." Her eyes twinkled as she talked. "'Mama, give me that filthy ring so I can clean it. You are a disgrace to my business,' he laughed. 'Wearing dirty jewelry is an insult to a jeweler.' He shook his head and walked out with the ring. I had no idea he was going to make me a new ring. He came in on Mother's Day morning with a big box and sat it on the kitchen table. 'Open it,' he said, looking like a six-year-old, a mischievous grin on his face. I stopped what I was doing, walked over to the table, and just stared at him. I asked what he'd gone and done now. I'd told him not to spend any money on me. 'Just open the box,' he said. I picked up the box and shook it. It felt light. I started opening it, and he looked so sweet watching me tear into his surprise. When I got the box unwrapped, there was another box, and then another, until finally I found a little tiny box. When I opened it, there was the most beautiful ring I had ever seen. I just cried. I took the ring out of the box, put it on my finger, and looked up at him. He looked so proud, and I was so proud of him my heart almost burst. He took my hands in his and said, "Mama, I appreciate all you have done for me. I know there were times you did without so that I could have something I wanted, like my first shotgun and my first truck. You cleaned houses for extra money to help me put a down payment on that '87 Chevy. Thank you, Mama; I love you, and I finally realize what it meant to have a mama like you all these years. Then he picked me up and swung me around." Scarlet laughed, reliving it just as if it had happened yesterday.

Scarlet felt someone standing behind her and turned to see who was there. It was Jason.

"Miss Scarlet, I stole your rings," he said. "I don't even know why I did it, but I am truly sorry I hurt you."

"Jason?" Scarlet looked at him in disbelief and then her face softened. "Jason, that doesn't matter anymore. The rings are back on my fingers where they belong, and that is all that we will say about it."

"Thank you, Miss Scarlet."

Scarlet walked over and put her arms around Jason. "It's okay, son. It's okay."

Jason stood still a moment and then slowly put his arms around Scarlet.

Melanie and Leona looked at each other in disbelief. Melanie whispered to Leona, "Must be a Christmas miracle."

Leona nodded.

"It's been a long day, and I am going to bed." Scarlet backed away from Jason and smiled at him. "Goodnight, Jason, and thank you for making Christmas special again."

"Yes, ma'am."

Scarlet left to go to her room, and Jason went to his. Melanie and Leona high-fived quietly.

"Things are looking up, wouldn't you say?" Melanie asked.

"I would say they are definitely looking up," said Leona.

"Let's get out of here and go home," Melanie laughed. "I haven't finished my shopping yet."

"I'm with you," Leona agreed. "I've got a terrible headache, and I plan to rest when I get home. Too much excitement around here, I guess."

"Are you okay to drive?" Melanie asked, concerned. Leona had been complaining of headaches a lot lately and had even mentioned being dizzy at times and seeing flashes of light.

"Sure, I'm okay. It's just a headache," Leona answered, unconcerned.

"Yeah, but you've had a lot of headaches lately. I think you should see a doctor. What about the dizziness and flashes of light you told me about?"

"I'm sure it's just stress," Leona answered. "You know I've had a lot on me lately with Tommy, and then there's Jim and his drinking."

Melanie noted the worry lines on Leona's face. She did have a lot on her. Her husband was an alcoholic, and her son Tommy had been caught using drugs. He was a great kid, but he was hanging around with the wrong crowd.

"I just want you to take care of yourself. You always take care of other people, and I don't know what I would do if anything happened to you." Melanie gave Leona a hug.

Leona smiled. "I'm okay, really."

"Okay, then. You're a nurse, and I take your word for it. Now, I really have to go. I'll see you tomorrow," Melanie said as she turned loose of Leona.

"Okay. Have a good night," Leona replied as they got into their cars.

Melanie still had not told Leona about the baby. She hadn't really wanted to talk about it. She knew Leona would be there for Morgan; there was no doubt about that. Still, she wanted to wait until after Christmas to tell anyone. She figured the fewer people that knew about it, the less chance the news would leak out before they were ready. Melanie felt she would never be ready, but ready or not, it was coming.

When Melanie got home, Morgan was lying on the couch, watching TV. Melanie walked over and patted her on the head. "Hungry?"

"Yes, I stay hungry now since I'm eating for two."

"Well, what would you like for supper?"

"It doesn't matter as long as it doesn't take long to fix."

"How about spaghetti?"

"Sounds good to me." Melanie went into the kitchen, and Morgan followed.

"Mama, I been thinking about the last name since we talked about it."

"And?"

"The baby's daddy wants me to use his last name."

"Are you planning on marrying him?"

"Don't know right now. Maybe one day."

"Why not just give the baby your last name, if you are not sure you're going to marry Daryl?"

"I don't know. Daryl would be upset if I did that."

"Well, Daryl should have thought about that before now."

"It's as much my fault as it is his, you know," she replied defensively.

"Yes, unfortunately, I do know. That makes it even worse. Morgan, think about this very carefully. His dad may not always be around, but you will. Remember what I said about it being much easier to relate a child to his mother if they have the same last name. Then other children won't ask why his mama is a Hutchins and his name is Saunders."

Morgan pondered on that for a while. Melanie finished the spaghetti, and they sat down to eat in silence, each in her own world. Melanie hoped Morgan would listen to her, but Daryl seemed to have more influence these days than she did. After they finished eating, Morgan went back to the couch, and Melanie finished cleaning the kitchen. She was bushed and went to her room to go to bed.

She had always relied on God to help her through difficult times, but she needed his guidance more and more these days. It had been a difficult year. As Melanie finished her prayers, she ended with, "As I was with Moses, so will I be with thee. I will not fail thee or forsake thee. Be strong and of good courage." (Joshua 1:5-6) Melanie said the verse several times, until she fell asleep.

Christmas Eve finally arrived, and Melanie was excited. She loved Christmas. She wrapped presents and sung Christmas songs to herself. Dinner went smoothly with Ron, Kevin, and Morgan. Kevin was on his best behavior. After dinner, when Kevin left and Morgan went to her room, she and Ron enjoyed a quiet glass of wine together before calling it a night. Melanie had decided not to invite Ron to Christmas with her family this year. She thought it was a little too soon for all that. She did think a lot of him already and hoped it would lead to something big, but with all that was going on with Morgan and Kevin she would be distracted, and she just didn't feel like having anything else on her plate.

As the day went on, Melanie couldn't help but think of all the changes about to take place. By next year this time, there would be a new baby in the house, her grandchild. A precious gift from God. In all honesty, she still wasn't sure how she felt about the biracial part of it. She wished the father were white, mostly because having a baby and not being married was big enough issue without having to throw in racial complications. It would be an issue with a lot of people. Morgan still had not told her daddy the news, and somehow, Melanie knew she would be the one to drop that bomb. They had to tell him right after Christmas.

She awoke Christmas morning as excited as if she were twelve years old again. Melanie loved Christmas. She wished she could go back in time and relive some of the happy Christmases, when her biggest worry was if Santa would leave the right doll for her. Strangely enough, he always did. She wondered how he kept all the little girls straight in his mind. She remembered her and her brother Charles planning to catch Santa putting toys under the tree, but they always ended up falling asleep before Santa arrived. They planned to take shifts to watch for him, but the next morning, when they awoke, the toys were under the tree, and Santa was gone. She smiled to herself as she peeped in on Morgan. Fast asleep. If she could just go back to when they were kids, she would be happy. The things she would do different. For one, there would never have been a divorce, and she would have spent more time with her children and making a happier home. Most of all, she would have taken them to church more. Oh, well, she thought. Too late to think about all that now. Kevin would be coming over soon to open presents and go to her parents' for the day. In the past few weeks, he seemed to be getting worse. Dan had told her about his mood swings and temper tantrums. At first, she thought Dan was exaggerating, but recently, she had seen evidence of it herself. She didn't understand what was going on with him, but she knew he was changing and needed help. It was up to her to find that help.

After opening their gifts, Morgan, Kevin, and she went to her parents' house for Christmas dinner. The big tree was surrounded by pretty presents waiting to put a smile on the receivers' faces. Christmas at her parents' was always fun, with lots of laughter and memories of Christmases past.

Melanie noted the loose-fitting denim shirt Morgan had on. Why doesn't she just tattoo "with child" on her forehead? It was a dead giveaway. Morgan never dressed like that. She was about four months pregnant, though, and really couldn't wear her clingy clothes any longer.

Everyone was home for Christmas; all the grandkids were there, including the great grandchild, incognito, in Morgan's womb. Melanie shivered at the thought. She prayed the secret she and Morgan were carrying would not destroy the close relationship she had with her family. Melanie's mama and daddy were getting older, and her daddy had been diagnosed with end-stage Parkinson's disease. It was taking a toll on his health. Melanie worried how the news of a biracial great grandchild might affect them. Even though she didn't go to church as much as she should have when she was growing up, she was raised in a Christian home, and being pregnant and unmarried was not the way it was supposed to be. Her parents had been married almost sixty years, and morals and values were very important to them. Her parents had set a good example for their family, yet she had let her own children down. She envied their longevity, and again was sad to know she would never celebrate a fiftieth wedding anniversary, as they had done a few years back.

Melanie put a smile on her face and acted as if everything was fine, as she had done many times before, when on the inside, she was terrified of the unknown. Some of those times, when she thought she had them fooled, her mama had asked her if everything was okay. Of course, Melanie always assured her everything was fine. She remembered a few times breaking down and crying when she was hugging her mama goodbye after a visit. She honestly couldn't explain the sudden outburst of tears, except that there's something about a mother's closeness that makes a child vulnerable, no matter what age the child is. Melanie tried to disguise the fear in her heart, hoping no one would guess the truth about what would rock their world, too.

Christmas day came and went with no questions asked. Even if they suspected Morgan's pregnancy, they would wait until she was ready to tell them. The biggest shock would not be the pregnancy, but the father. Melanie wanted to tell Joan first. Melanie always cried on Joan's shoulder as if she were the older sister, when actually, she was six years younger. Joan always gave her honest opinion if she asked for it, and a few times when she hadn't, especially when she was dating James. She, and the rest of her family, had not liked James at all and only tolerated him for her sake. Above all, Joan was a true Christian and would not judge Morgan for her actions. Right now, Melanie needed someone that would not judge Morgan, but would be there to support both of them, and she knew Joan would. She had always been there for her. When she was going through her divorce, she had gotten a card in the mail every day for weeks from Joan encouraging her, telling her to be strong. Sometimes it would be a humorous card and make Melanie burst out laughing, when moments before she had felt like crying. Sometimes, after reading the card, she would shake her head, wondering how a card could have such perfect timing. The thoughts brought a smile to Melanie's face. She would call Joan next week and ask her to lunch then drop the bombshell on her before proceeding with the rest of the family.

Chapter Eleven

$\mathcal{M}$elanie went to work on Monday, ready to head into a new year. Melanie ran into Scarlet in the kitchen as she went to get her morning coffee.

Scarlet was smiling. "I am going home today."

"That is wonderful, Scarlet. I know you can hardly wait."

"Yes, I am very excited. I have plenty to do around there to keep that big place up."

"I'm sure you do."

"Yes, I can't wait to get home. Although I must admit, this stay has been a big help. I feel much better about myself, and I'm not depressed like I was. Dr. Williams is an excellent doctor, and all the staff has been so nice. It is almost like a family. I have gotten attached to so many of the people here, especially you."

"Well, thank you, Scarlet. We have gotten very fond of you, also, and will miss the ray of sunshine that you bring to us each day."

"There is another person I have gotten attached to and will miss."

"Oh, yeah? Who might that be?"

"Jason." Scarlet smiled. "Yes, I will miss that young fellow, too."

"Oh, really?"

"I hope he will be okay. I know he doesn't have any family left—just like me."

Melanie's brain suddenly clicked. She doesn't have family; he doesn't have family. Why not be each other's family? Hm, I might be on to something here.

"Scarlet," Melanie started hesitantly, thinking of how to plant the idea.

"Yes?"

"Why don't you offer Jason a place to stay at your house in return for doing some work around there? You said earlier it was a big place to keep up. Couldn't you use some help?"

"Well, I don't know. I guess I could use some help. But I'm sure he wouldn't want to come live in the country with an old lady like me."

"Would you be willing to see if he is interested?" Melanie asked anxiously.

"I suppose so," she said, narrowing her eyes as if weighing the thought in her mind.

"Good. Then I will tell Dr. Williams that when Jason is ready for discharge, he does have somewhere to go."

Scarlet smiled. "Yes, that would be just fine with me. In fact, I rather like the idea very much. I like the idea so much, that when he is ready for discharge, I will come back and make the offer myself, if it is okay with Dr. Williams."

"Great!" Melanie jumped up and hugged Scarlet. They both laughed as they embraced.

Scarlet went to her room to pack her things. As she was packing, Jason walked by the door and then backed up to peep in.

"Ms. Scarlet?"

Scarlet turned to see Jason standing in the door. "Hi, Jason."

"Ms. Scarlet, why are you packing?"

"I am going home today."

"Today?" he asked, surprised.

"Yes, son. Today. I am so excited. I can hardly wait to get home to my garden. I also have goats, two dogs, three cats, and four kittens. I need to be there. I am sure they missed me."

"Oh, I see." Jason looked down and kicked at the door jam, trying not to show his disappointment. "Well, Ms. Scarlet, I wish you the best," Jason said sincerely.

"Thank you, son. I will miss you and the others." Scarlet wanted to tell him about the conversation she'd had earlier with Melanie, but she had promised not to say anything until Melanie mentioned it to Dr. Williams. "Jason, I'm sure you will be going home soon, too."

"Home? Where is home? I have no home." Jason looked a little embarrassed then. It was almost as if he didn't want anyone to know he had feelings and that those feelings were hurting.

Scarlet walked over to Jason, took his face in her hands, and looked him in the eyes. "I am sure something will work out for you. You hear me? You know the old saying 'Never give up?' That is going to be my new motto, and I want it to be yours, too." She kissed him on the cheek. "Now, let me see those dimples."

Strangely enough, Jason smiled. "Ms. Scarlet, I wish you good luck and hope to meet you again one day"

"Jason, I'm sure we will meet again," she said kindly, smiling.

Jason backed out of the room, and Scarlet turned to finish packing with a grin on her face. She had a secret—a secret she hoped would change both of their lives for the better.

Dr. Williams came in for his morning appointments. Tawanna was the first appointment for the day. He looked at her and asked if she had done what he told her to do at their last meeting.

"Yes, I did," she answered coolly.

"Then, please, share it with me," Dr. Williams said softly.

"You ask me to write down all the reasons I should keep the baby and all the reasons I should not keep the baby." She hesitated.

"Go on."

"Well, there is only one list."

"And?"

"The list not to keep the baby."

"And why is that, Tawanna?"

"There are no good reasons to keep this baby."

"Okay, can we go a little further with the reasons?"

"I want to give the baby up for adoption."

"Adoption?" Dr. Williams said, his eyes widening in surprise.

"Yes."

"Have you thought of other alternatives, like letting your parents raise the child? I'm sure they would not want to give their grandchild up for adoption," Dr. Williams said seriously.

"Can't."

"Why not?"

Tawanna's eyes were filled with tears. "I can't tell you."

"Tawanna, I am here to help you, not judge you," Dr. Williams said.

"I know."

"Please, trust me."

"I do trust you, but it is very complicated and will hurt a lot of people."

"I told you; you are not the first young girl to get pregnant, and the young man should take some responsibility, too," Dr. Williams urged.

Tawanna turned her face. "It's not what you think," she said, her voice cracking.

"Then what is it?" Dr. Williams touched her arm gently. "You can tell me."

"No, I can't tell you. I would rather die first."

"Tawanna, please don't say that."

"I would. I would rather be dead than for anyone to know the truth." Tawanna jumped up and ran out of the room.

Dr. Williams just sat there for a moment, trying to figure it out. He shook his head and threw up his hands. "I have seen a lot of young, pregnant girls in my career, and they were upset, but nothing like this. She is overly sensitive, and I need to help her before she breaks. I am really worried about her. I will see her again tomorrow. I have got to get through to her somehow. Something is eating at her, and it is about to destroy her. She is on the verge of a nervous breakdown." Dr. Williams got up and walked out of the room, still trying to unravel the mystery.

"Dr. William! Dr. Williams!" It was Scarlet.

Dr. Williams smiled as he turned and walked towards Scarlet. "Yes, my pretty lady, what may I do for you today?"

Scarlet smiled, loving the compliment. "I wanted to talk to you about something in private." She took Dr. Williams by the hand, led him to her room, and closed the door.

"Dr. Williams, I was talking with Melanie earlier today, and we had an idea that we wanted your opinion on."

"Okay, you have my attention."

"We were thinking that maybe when Jason was ready to be discharged, he could come live with me and help me take care of the farm in return."

Dr. William's face lit up. "Scarlet, I think that would be a great idea."

"You do?" she said, surprised he had agreed so easily.

"Yes, I really do. I think it would be good for Jason, and I think it would be good for you, too."

"Then, it's settled. When he's ready, I will make him an offer."

"Good for you. He'd be a fool not to jump at it." Dr. Williams smiled at Scarlet. "You are a super lady."

"Thanks." Scarlet beamed like he had never seen before.

"I will miss you around here," Dr Williams teased.

"And I will miss all of you. Thank you, doctor, for all you have done. I will never forget you."

Dr. Williams put his arm around Scarlet's shoulder as they walked out of the room. "As much as I enjoyed your company, I don't want to see you back here, okay?"

"Okay, I promise I won't be back," she answered, still smiling.

"Good deal."

"Bye, Doc."

"Goodbye, pretty lady," Dr. Williams said softly as he kissed her on the cheek. "You take care of yourself."

Scarlet watched Dr. Williams walk away, then mumbled, "If that man wasn't married..." and grinned to herself. It was the first time since her husband deserted her that she had looked at man in that way. She turned to go back to her room to finish packing. She was really happy for the first time in a long while. It was a good feeling.

The next few days were pretty uneventful. Melanie still had not told anyone about Morgan. She had to tell Dan, but she was not looking forward to it. Even Morgan had said it might give him a heart attack. Melanie didn't think it would kill him, but she was afraid he might want to kill Morgan. Not literally, but almost.

It just so happened that Dan stopped by that afternoon to check something on Morgan's car. When he got to his truck to leave, Melanie decided to tell him before someone else did.

Melanie took a deep breath. "Dan, there is something I need to talk to you about."

"What?" he said abruptly.

"It's about Morgan." She hesitated, trying to brace herself for what was about to come.

He stared and waited.

"Morgan is pregnant," she blurted. There. It was out, and there was no taking it back.

His expression changed, the vein in his neck swelling. Maybe Morgan was right; maybe he was going to have a heart attack.

"Damn it!" He shook his head in disgust. "Well, she has ruined her life! Who is the daddy? Is he black?"

"I don't know him, only his name." She hesitated. "And yes, he is black."

She winced as if that would help close her ears, but it didn't.

"Damn it! I knew this would happen! Well, she will just have to have an abortion!"

He was angrier than Melanie had ever seen him, and she had seen him pretty angry during the divorce.

"She is not going to have an abortion," Melanie said, going in for the next round.

"Yes, she will! She has to! She can't have a black baby!" he said loudly.

His face had turned crimson red, and his hands had made fists, as if he were going to hit something. She was glad the young black man was nowhere around because as irate as Dan was, he probably would have hit him.

Melanie went on, in spite of his reaction. "She will not have an abortion. We have already talked about that, and she is determined to have the baby. Besides, it's too late for that now. She kept it a secret so no one could force her to have an abortion. She is nineteen years old, and she has a right to make her own decision, regardless of what you or the world thinks. She wants the baby, and she going to have it," Melanie said, all in one breath, before Dan had time to interrupt.

"Well, you tell her I am not going to have anything to do with her or the baby, and not to bring that black baby to my house, ever. I am cutting her out of my will. She won't get anything I have," he said firmly, his hands still in fists.

"Listen to me," Melanie said, angry. "That is your daughter in there."

"Not any more."

"Like it or not, we have to deal with it," Melanie continued.

"I'm taking the car I gave her back," he said.

"What good will that do?" she asked angrily. He could always light her fuse, and he was doing a good job of it now. He never was one she could discuss things with calmly; he always had to make bad matters even worse.

"None, but she doesn't deserve a car. She's stupid. How's a white girl going to raise a half-black baby in this town?" he said bitterly. The vein in his neck bulged, and his face was red.

Melanie knew he would not listen to anything she had to say, so she moved back from the vehicle, and he started the motor.

"I'm going to come get her car tomorrow!" Dan said, backing up.

Melanie threw up her hands. "Fine! Come get the car! Leave it all on me to handle!"

That was always the way he handled things with the kids. He turned his back; it was easier than staying and facing the truth. He had done the same thing with Kevin.

He backed out of the driveway and spun his wheels, throwing gravel everywhere when he left. Melanie stood there a moment looking at the black tire tracks as he screeched out of sight. "Well, that went well," she said sarcastically.

She turned to go to the house and caught a glimpse of Morgan in the upstairs bedroom window looking down at her. She was crying. Melanie hoped she had not heard her father's harsh words.

Morgan met her at the back door. "Judging by the way Daddy left, I suppose you told him I'm pregnant," she said, raising her eyebrows.

"You got it," Melanie answered.

"So what did he say?" she asked.

"Do you want the censored version or the uncensored version?" Melanie asked, still a little shaken by the ordeal.

"That bad, huh?" Morgan asked quietly.

"He said he is going to take your car and cut you out of his will," Melanie answered, disgusted.

Morgan stared. "My car?"

"Afraid so. Tomorrow, in fact."

Morgan got angry. "What am I going to do without my car? How am I going to get to work?"

"Don't know, and I guess Aunt Jenny will know you're pregnant now, so you don't have to worry about hiding your poochy stomach at the book store any more."

Morgan slammed her fist on the table. "That's just great! I guess I just won't go to work. How can he give me a car for my birthday and then take it back when he wants? That's insane! I'm nineteen years old, not twelve!" she yelled. Morgan ran to her room and slammed the door.

Not twelve? That is exactly what a twelve-year-old would do, Melanie thought, shaking her head in disbelief. She understood Morgan's frustration, and in all fairness, she understood Dan's frustration. Melanie knew he was reacting to the way other people would react to the news. Dan was well thought of in the community, and he did not want the embarrassment Morgan was about to bring him and his family. His sister Jenny owned the Christian book store where Morgan worked, and she would not be pleased with Morgan being pregnant and unmarried, but Melanie knew Jenny would not hurt Morgan's feelings deliberately.

Melanie heard things slamming in Morgan's room. She didn't dare try to talk to her now. It was best to let her vent a while then she would be rational, but not right now. She might get hit by a flying book or something.

Melanie felt helpless. She sat down at the kitchen table, laid her head on the table, and started to cry. She didn't know exactly how to handle this. After a few moments of feeling sorry for herself, she pulled herself together, wiped her face, and realized she had to be strong for Morgan. She could not let her go through this alone. Melanie was not happy about the situation, but she could not just throw up her hands and walk away from her daughter, either. The way Melanie saw it, she had two choices; she could continue to have the daughter she had always loved, or she could turn her back on Morgan. To Melanie, the choice was simple; she chose to keep her daughter. Melanie knew Dan loved Morgan as much as she did, and with time, he would accept Morgan's child and love it, too. He probably didn't think so right now, but Melanie knew he would come around eventually. In the mean time, he was going to make both their lives hell. For the next few months, he would rip and roar like a lion. Melanie prayed when he looked that little baby in the face, his heart would change.

Morgan needed some time alone, so Melanie did not go up to her room. Instead, she started fixing supper. When supper was ready, she went to Morgan's room and knocked on the door. Morgan was lying down. Melanie sat on the bed and rubbed Morgan's hair. When she was young, Morgan would lie next to Melanie and ask her to rub her head; now it had become, "Mama, will you rub my back? It hurts."

"Come on; let's go down and eat some supper," Melanie said gently.

Morgan looked up, her nose and eyes red from crying. "I don't want anything."

"Come on; you have to eat something. You are eating for two now."

"I heard what Daddy said. I heard what he called my baby."

"I'm sorry you heard that," Melanie said, still rubbing Morgan's head.

"I am not going to have an abortion, Mama."

"I know that," Melanie answered.

"I want this baby. I want someone all my own to love and to love me."

Again, Melanie couldn't help but wonder why Morgan had such a need to have someone love her. Didn't she know she loved her and would give her life for her? Had the divorce had such an impact on her life? Where had she failed? Had she been so selfish that her daughter had suffered the consequences? Too many questions, and Melanie didn't have any of the answers.

"Morgan, come on. I don't want to eat alone."

Morgan got up and wiped her eyes. Melanie handed her a tissue, and she blew her nose.

"Come on; I have fried chicken, one of your favorites."

Morgan forced a smile and followed Melanie to the kitchen. For the most part, they ate in silence, each deep in her thoughts.

When they finished eating, Morgan headed back up to her room and to the phone, no doubt to call her boyfriend and tell him all about her disownment and losing her car.

Melanie finished cleaning the kitchen and headed up to bed. She was exhausted. The mental strain was wearing on her. She lay in bed, thinking, "One down. How many to go?" Telling her family would not be easy, either. She prayed for strength for Morgan and for her unborn grandchild. She was still praying when she fell asleep.

The next day, Dan carried through with his threat to take Morgan's car. They were in the house when they heard Morgan's car start. Melanie looked at Morgan, and Morgan stared, frozen, knowing what was happening.

"I can't believe Daddy is taking my car!" she yelled. Morgan jumped from the couch and ran to the back door. Before she could get the door open, Dan drove out of the yard in Morgan's car. Morgan was in tears. "He stole my freaking car," she said in disbelief, throwing up her hands. "My own daddy stole my car. How's that going to look on the police report?"

"Unfortunately, dear, technically, it is his car. He paid for it, and it is in his name; therefore, he didn't steal it, he just took what was already his," Melanie said.

"He gave it to me for my birthday," Morgan corrected her.

"That is true," Melanie answered. "He did give it to you for your birthday, but it is still in his name, and by law it belongs to him."

Morgan didn't care about the law; she just could not relate to her daddy taking her car after he had given it to her. Melanie didn't know why she was so surprised; he had threatened to do it before when he heard she was seeing a black boy.

"I wish I was dead then everyone would be happy!" Morgan cried. "I wish my baby and I were gone from here." Morgan ran up to her room and slammed the door. The words stung Melanie's heart. Morgan was frustrated, but for her to say she wish she were dead was more than Melanie could stand.

Melanie couldn't handle it anymore, either; she grabbed her purse and car keys. She had to get away and calm down. She always felt like she was in the middle of everything with Dan and the kids. She was in the middle with Kevin, and now she was in the middle with Morgan. It would have been much easier to bear if she had a husband to lean on and say, "We'll get through this together, honey." Instead, she felt Dan always blamed her for the children's problems. Whenever they did anything wrong, the first thing out of his mouth was, "You're just like your mama." He had told Kevin and Morgan that more times than she could remember. Unfortunately, he didn't mean it as a compliment.

Tears burned Melanie's eyes as she backed out of the yard. Where was she going? She didn't know. It didn't matter; she just had to get away for a few minutes. She wanted to call Joan and talk to her, as she often did when she was upset about something, but Joan didn't know about the pregnancy yet, and she didn't want to tell her on the phone. Instead, she just drove around, alone, thinking. When her children were hurting, Melanie always thought the same thoughts; if only she could make them little again, she would. When they skinned their knees, she could fix it, when they had a cold she could fix it; when they had a bad dream, she was there to put her arms around them so they could feel safe and go back to sleep, but now she felt helpless. She couldn't fix Kevin's brain injury, and she couldn't fix Morgan's life or her feelings of rejection and disgrace. Tears burned her eyes as she again thought of Morgan's words. "I wish I was dead."

Melanie pulled the car over and stopped. She leaned her head over on the steering wheel and let it out, crying as if her heart were breaking. I failed the two people I love more than anything in the world. I can't fix them anymore. I can't even fix me. Melanie did the only thing she knew to do—she started to pray.

"I don't know the answers, God. Please show me the way to help Kevin and Morgan. I know you gave your son for me, but I am begging you to help my son. Oh, God! Please help me." Melanie prayed for Morgan and her unborn child and begged for his guidance. She didn't know where to go or what to do, but she believed He would lead her in the right direction. Melanie kept saying over and over, "I believe, and I know you will show me the way to help Kevin and Morgan." Melanie ended by saying, as she always did, "Thank you, God, for all my blessings."

Melanie sat up and wiped her face. She knew she was blessed because Kevin's life had been spared, and even though he wasn't like he was before the accident, she still had him and could put her arms around him, and she could still hear him say, "I love you, Mama." Melanie also knew that Morgan's baby was a blessing and that God had a purpose for that, too. Melanie felt better after her cry and talk with God. She felt she could go back and face the situation with more courage. Melanie started the car and headed for home, ready once again to be the support her kids counted on. She would not let them down again.

The next morning, Melanie called Joan and asked if they could meet for lunch in Williamston. Williamston was about halfway for both, and they occasionally met there for lunch. Joan agreed, and Melanie told her she would be there around noon. When Joan arrived, Melanie was sitting in her car wondering how she would spring the news about Morgan. She had rehearsed it in her mind, and even though she knew Joan would be there for her, she dreaded telling her.

Joan was smiling as she got out of the car and came over to hug Melanie. "This is a pleasant surprise."

"Yeah, I know."

Joan could read her like a book, and it didn't take but a minute for her to see something was on Melanie's mind. They went into the little café, and Melanie picked a table in the corner by the window, away from the few other customers.

Joan followed. "Are you okay?"

The waitress came to get their drink order, and Melanie ordered a glass of wine, something she rarely did for lunch.

Joan looked at her. "Must be a bad day," she teased.

"A bad year—no, make that years."

Joan smiled sympathetically. "Well, I know it's something."

Melanie didn't know where to begin. "I don't know why my life has to be so complicated. Just when one thing begins to straighten out, something else falls apart. First, there was the divorce, right while I was in nursing school, and I barely got through that. Then there was Kevin's accident, and I'll never get over that, and now there's Morgan."

Joan looked at Melanie with sudden concern. "Is she okay? What is wrong with her? Is she sick?"

"She's okay," Melanie said, putting her hand on Joan's arm to calm her.

The waitress brought their drinks, and Melanie took a swallow of her wine and slowly put the glass down, staring at it a moment as her hands nervously played with the stem of the glass.

"She's not sick." The words stuck in Melanie's throat as she tried to get the rest of her sentence out. "She's pregnant." Melanie picked up the wine glass and took another sip.

"Oh, honey; I'm sorry," Joan said, patting Melanie on the hand.

"Me too."

Melanie dreaded the next part even more. She swirled the wine around in the glass slowly. Joan watched Melanie play with the glass of wine. Melanie picked up the glass and took another swallow.

"That's not all," Melanie said, looking at Joan.

Joan waited for her to continue. "What?"

Melanie hesitated, and Joan waited patiently.

"The daddy…"

"The daddy what? Doesn't want to marry her?" Joan asked.

"The daddy…" Melanie hesitated again and then looked into Joan's face. "The daddy is black," Melanie said quietly, looking around to see if anyone had heard.

Joan was shocked, but she held her emotions well. Her facial expression barely changed.

"Oh, no," she said softly, looking at Melanie. She picked up Melanie's glass of wine, took a swallow, and handed it back to Melanie. Melanie smiled briefly; Joan didn't drink wine. "Who is the father?"

"Some boy she went to school with. I think she has been seeing him for a while, but I refused to believe it."

"You had heard."

"Dan told me he had heard a rumor that Morgan had been seen riding with a black boy in her car, but that didn't mean anything to me. Morgan's always had black friends. I mean, she was in every sport in high school and was constantly around black boys. They were all her friends."

"That's true," Joan agreed.

"She's not going to have an abortion, and I support her decision on that. I have never agreed with abortion."

"Good for her," Joan agreed. "What about marriage?"

"I don't know; we haven't even discussed that. What if I can't love my own grandchild?" Melanie asked, getting to the heart of the matter, looking at Joan as her eyes swelled with water.

"You will love that child, no matter who the daddy is," Joan said firmly. "Any child is a gift from God, and there's nowhere in the Bible that says having a child by another race is a sin. In fact, Moses married a woman of another race; there were many interracial marriages in the Bible. The Bible does speak against marrying outside your religion, and many people confuse that with interracial marriage. Yes, she should have gotten married first, but in God's eyes, race doesn't matter. Listen to me, Mel; when that baby is born, you will have no problem loving it. We will all love it, and we will all be here to support her. I know it's hard, and you've been dealt some hard knocks, but you will make it through this. I know you."

Melanie smiled. "Thanks. I haven't told Mama and Daddy or Charles yet."

"I know telling Mama and Daddy will probably be the hardest," Joan said.

"Yes, it will. I feel like I'm always the carrier of bad news. As the old saying goes, I guess I'm the only hell my Mama and Daddy ever raised."

Joan shook her head. "No, I told you; you've just been dealt some hard knocks, and they know that. I'm not going to lie. I know it's going to hurt them, but they'll never turn their backs on you or Morgan or the baby."

"I know, but I feel like the family misfit."

"You are not!" Joan said, smiling, shaking her head.

Melanie took the last swallow of the wine and set the glass down. "Well, I guess I'll go tell Mama and Daddy next. I wanted to tell you first. The only other person I have told is Dan."

Joan shrugged. "How did that go over?"

"Well, he disowned her and took her car away, for starters."

"Her car! Why her car?"

"You know Dan. He giveth and he taketh away," Melanie said.

Joan shrugged her shoulders. "Evidently."

"Well, I guess I better go get it over with. Thanks for coming to meet me."

"Do you want me to go with you?"

"No, I'd rather do it alone."

"You know I'm here for you and Morgan," Joan said.

"I know, and I appreciate it more than you know," Melanie said.

They walked out to their cars, and Joan hugged Melanie. "Call me if you need me."

"Ring, ring; I need you," Melanie said, trying to smile.

Joan laughed. "I mean it, and tell Morgan I'm here for her, too."

"Thanks. I love you a bunch," Melanie said, getting in her car.

"I love you, too, and take care of yourself."

Melanie nodded, shutting the car door. Melanie sighed. "One down. How many more to go?" she said as she pulled out of the parking lot.

Melanie picked up her cell phone, called her mother, and told her she was coming over later that afternoon. Her mother was excited and said she would fry some chicken for supper.

When Melanie arrived at her parents' house, her mama met her at the door and gave her a hug then led Melanie to the living room, where her daddy was in his recliner. He sat the recliner up and waited for his hug. Melanie smiled at him and hugged him, dreading the news she was about to burden on them. When Kevin got hurt, it almost killed them worrying about him.

Melanie sat down and talked with her parents for a few minutes about the weather, neighbors, and family chit-chat. Her mother went to the kitchen to set the table, and as usual, it was a full spread—fired chicken, butter beans, candied yams, corn, biscuits, and tea. On the counter was a freshly-baked lemon pie. Her mother loved taking care of her family and cooking for them. Even though it was only the two of them, she still cooked a full meal every day. Her daddy sat across from her, and her mama sat at the end of the kitchen table. Melanie's appetite was not what it would have ordinarily been. Her mama encouraged her daddy to eat, as she always did. He put small amounts of food on his plate, but her mama had to coax him to eat even that.

After they finished eating, Melanie sat there, dreading bringing up Morgan and the pregnancy. After a few minutes, Melanie decided she had to tell them, and it was not going to get any easier. In fact, it was getting harder.

"I have something to tell you, and it's not easy for me to say."

Her mama looked at her and waited. Her daddy sipped his coffee and then looked up at Melanie.

"It's Morgan. She's pregnant."

Her mama looked at her, waiting to hear the rest. Her daddy looked away, picked up his coffee cup, and took another sip.

"That's not all."

Neither of them said a word as they waited for Melanie to continue.

"The father is black." Melanie dropped her head.

"Oh, my goodness," her mother said in almost a whisper, putting her hand over her mouth and resting her elbow on the table as she stared at Melanie.

Her daddy never spoke. He shook his head slowly looking down into his half-empty plate. Melanie told them about Morgan's pregnancy and her plans to keep the baby, Dan's reaction, her own disappointment, and that no matter what, she would be there for Morgan. Her mama had tears in her eyes, and her daddy stared sadly at his coffee cup then picked it up, took another swallow, and set it back down quietly.

"I'm so sorry." Tears spilled over on Melanie's cheeks. "I know it's a shock, and it's your first great-grandchild. If I could undo it I would, but I can't."

For a moment they just sat there. Tears trickled down her mama's cheek, and she quickly wiped it away with her napkin. Finally, she spoke. "Of course we're disappointed, but we love Morgan, and we're not going to turn our backs on her or her child. She will always be welcome here, you know that."

Melanie smiled, shaking her head, "I know."

Her daddy never said a word, but he rarely did about those kinds of things. He wouldn't hurt her feelings, and that's probably why he didn't say anything. He was disappointed. She could see it on his face. Melanie got up and started cleaning the table.

"I can do this," her mama insisted. "I want you to get home before dark. You know I worry about you being on the road by yourself at night."

Melanie was emotionally drained and decided to take her up on her offer. She hugged her mama tight and said softly, "I'm sorry." Her voice broke with emotion.

"I'm sorry for you. You take care of yourself; you're the one I worry about. You're my child, remember?"

Melanie smiled through her tears and went to where her daddy was still sitting at the table quietly watching them. She hugged him gently. "I'll see ya next time."

"Okay," he said. "Hurry back."

Melanie smiled, wiping her eyes and nose. "I'll call you," she told her mama.

"Okay," she said, looking at Melanie, concerned. "I wish I could help you."

"You have," Melanie said, hugging her mama tightly. She turned and walked out the door, not wanting them to see her crying. Melanie got into the car and let the tears go. She cried so hard she could hardly see the driveway. She knew how hurt her parents were, but was proud of them for the way they handled the news. They hadn't over reacted, hadn't made a scene, and hadn't scorned Morgan. She wasn't surprised; it was the way they had been all her life—supportive, loving, and family-oriented. Her family was her greatest blessing, and she knew it.

Melanie drove home thinking about Morgan and the baby. She would call Charles when she got home; maybe by then her emotions would be a little more settled.

When she got home, she picked up the phone and dialed Charles' number. As it rang, she practiced what she was going to say one more time. It couldn't be as hard as telling her parents, she thought.

"Hello?"

"Hi, Charles. How are you doing?"

"Okay. And you?"

"Okay, I guess. Look, there's something I need to tell you."

Charles understood, as she knew he would. They had always been close, and he had worried about her since her divorce from Dan. Charles told her he loved her and to tell Morgan he loved her, too, and if there was any way he could help, let him know. When Melanie hung up the phone, she took a deep breath and let it out with a long sigh.

She had been dreading telling her family since before Christmas. They all knew now, and it felt like a burden had been lifted from her shoulders. Now she felt she could face the rest of the world because none of them mattered as much as the people she had told today and all of them were there to support her.

The next couple of weeks passed quickly. Melanie saw more of Ron and felt she had finally found someone she could love, and just maybe he loved her, too. He seemed to like Morgan a lot, and Morgan seemed to like him. Ron was so easy-going. Any old thing was okay. She had never met anyone so even tempered. Even though he was not a man for a lot of compliments, he never criticized her. Melanie liked that part a lot. The not-criticizing part—since most of the men in her life had enjoyed putting her down and hurting her feelings.

Chapter Twelve

*D*r. Williams would be releasing Jason soon. Melanie was concerned about what would happen to him when he left. Today they would talk to him about his options. His options were limited. They would tell him about Scarlet's offer to live with her, or he could go back to living on the streets. To Melanie, the choice was simple, but she did not know what Jason might choose.

Dr. Williams told Leona to bring Jason to his office. Jason knocked on the door lightly.

"Come in."

"Dr. Williams, I understand you want to see me."

"Yes, Jason. Come in and have a seat."

Dr. Williams finished what he was doing and set the papers aside. "Jason, you are ready to be discharged."

"I am?"

"Yes, son; it is time for you to go. Now the question is— where are you going?"

Jason stared at him, as if being released was totally a surprise.

"You knew this day was coming. Haven't you thought about what you wanted to do?"

"Dr. Williams, I don't know. I don't have any family. I don't have a job. I don't have a home, and I don't even have any friends that are straight."

"Then forget about them. You certainly don't need to get involved in drugs and alcohol again."

Jason leaned forward, rested his elbows on Dr. Williams' desk, and propped his chin on his hands, staring at Dr. Williams. "Doc, I don't know. Do you have any suggestions?"

"Well, son, I was hoping you would ask me that. As a matter of fact, I do have a suggestion."

Jason opened his eyes wide and his eyebrows arched. "You do?"

"Yes, I do." Dr. Williams smiled.

"What is it?"

"Jason, you are in luck."

"How's that, Doc?" Jason asked, confused, his elbows still propped on Dr. Williams desk, his head still propped on his hands.

"I tell you what, why don't I let someone else tell you?" Dr. Williams said.

Jason looked confused.

"Leona, would you please tell Melanie to send the person waiting in her office to my office now?"

"Yes, sir, I will." Leona grinned as she paged Melanie's office. "Melanie, Dr. Williams is ready."

In a few moments, there was a tap on Dr. Williams' door. Dr. Williams stood and went to the door and opened it.

"Come in, pretty lady. It's good to see you again. You are looking prettier than ever," Dr. Williams told Scarlet.

Scarlet put her arms around Dr. Williams and hugged him tight. "Hi, Doc. Flattery will get you anywhere," she said, winking at him.

Dr. Williams smiled and turned to Jason, who was just watching, waiting to see what Scarlet had to do with him. Why was she here? He had to admit he was glad to see her again, and he felt a warm feeling inside when he saw her.

Scarlet walked over to Jason and gave him a big hug. "My, my, boy, you need to eat a few biscuits; you are getting too skinny. You feel like a bag of bones."

Jason smiled.

"Scarlet, would you like to tell Jason why you are here?"

"Sure." Scarlet sat down in front of Jason and took his hands in hers. "Jason, I am here to make you an offer." She paused for a second, looking at Jason for some kind of reaction.

Jason, sat quietly, looking at Scarlet, waiting to hear what she had to say.

Scarlet continued, "It seems to me that we need each other. You need a place to live, and I need someone to help me on the farm." Scarlet paused again.

It was obvious Jason was shocked, judging by the look on his face. Scarlet couldn't tell if it was a good shock or a bad shock, so she continued. "I would like it very much if you would come live with me."

Jason looked bewildered. His lips started to curve upward, and he broke into a big smile.

"Are you for real?" he said when he finally found his voice. For a moment, he was actually speechless.

"I am for very real," Scarlet laughed.

"Ms. Scarlet, I can't believe this is happening."

"It's happening. So what do you think, Jason? Are you interested in coming to live with me and working on the farm? I must tell you, farm work is not easy."

Jason looked at Dr. Williams and then back to Scarlet, still smiling. "Yes, Ms. Scarlet, I would love to come live with you on the farm."

"Well, then, it's settled." Scarlet looked at Dr. Williams. "When will he be ready to leave this dump? No offense, Doc," Scarlet said, laughing.

Dr. Williams broke into a big laugh. "Is now soon enough?"

"I guess it is," she said. She turned to Jason. "Go pack your things. We're out of here."

Jason smiled. "That won't take long. I don't have anything but a jacket, a couple pair of jeans, and a couple of tee shirts."

"Well, get 'em and let's go. We got places to go and things to do." She winked at Jason.

Jason jumped up and headed out. He stopped at the door and turned around. "Doc?"

"Yes, Jason?"

"I just want to thank you for all you have done for me. I wouldn't have made it if you hadn't helped me."

Dr. Williams stood, walked over to Jason, and stuck out his hand. Jason grabbed his hand and shook it firmly. Jason hugged Dr. Williams' neck with his other arm, still holding the hand-shake.

Dr. Williams patted Jason on the back. "It was my pleasure to help such a fine young man. I'm sure you will do just fine in your new life. You said goodbye to the old; now it is time to start over."

"Yes, sir. I know that now."

"Take care, Jason, and take good care of this pretty lady."

"I will, Doc. I will."

Jason left the room, and Dr. Williams turned to Scarlet. "You are a very special lady, and I wish you and Jason the best. I think this is going to work really well for both of you. He is a fine young man that's had a really bad break in life. He will be fine now that he has let go of the guilt and the anger. You are just what he needs."

"Thank you, Doc. I know it is going to be a good thing. I have a gut feeling, and my gut feelings are always right. Thank you again. I will never forget your kindness." Scarlet walked to the door and gave Dr. Williams a hug goodbye. "Take care, Doc."

"You, too, pretty lady."

Scarlet smiled. Jason was already waiting for her with his little plastic bag of belongings.

"Bye, everyone, take care," Jason hollered as he was going to the door. Other residents turned and waved goodbye.

Melanie was at her desk, and she got up and walked over to Jason and Scarlet. "Well, well, well. Why are you two beaming so?"

"I'm going home with Ms. Scarlet," Jason said proudly.

Yes, I heard." Melanie hugged Jason goodbye. "Good luck, Jason."

"Thanks, Ms. Melanie."

"You're welcome. Now, go!"

"Yes, ma'am."

Melanie hugged Scarlet. "Good luck to you, too," Melanie whispered as she hugged Scarlet's neck.

"Thanks. I think my luck has changed. I am feeling blessed."

"Good. Take care and let us hear from the two of you."

"We will," Scarlet said.

Jason opened the door and motioned for Scarlet to go ahead of him. "Age before beauty," he teased.

Scarlet laughed and shook her head. "I believe that saying is beauty before beast." She grinned.

He laughed as he shut the door behind them.

Melanie walked to the side window to watch Scarlet and Jason walk to the parking lot. They were laughing and talking as they walked, Jason carrying his little plastic bag of clothes. Melanie couldn't believe her eyes as Scarlet lead Jason to a royal blue '87 souped-up Chevy truck. Jason's face lit up when Scarlet threw him the keys. She walked to the other side of the truck and got in. Melanie smiled and waved Dr. Williams and some of the other staff over to see the truck that had belonged to Scarlet's son. As they pulled out of the parking lot, they saw the shiny new license plate, 2NDCHANC, as it slowly left the parking lot. The truck turned onto the highway, headed for the country. Jason mashed down on the gas, and the dual exhaust roared. The two of them laughed as they took off down the highway. Melanie had a lump in her throat as she watched the truck disappear.

Dr. Williams laughed as he turned and walked away. "Some things around here do have a happy ending," Dr. Williams said, smiling, as he walked into his office and shut the door.

Melanie felt really good about the pair that had just left. She truly felt their lives had been blessed by coming in contact with one another at Eastside Medical. She hoped they stayed in touch. This time the ending had been good. She wished all endings could be that happy.

Chapter Thirteen

When Melanie got home that afternoon, Morgan was lying on the couch. It was odd to see her with a swollen stomach after seeing her with almost a perfect figure all her teen years. Melanie was sure it was an adjustment for Morgan, as well. She now looked like she had swallowed a watermelon, as the old saying went. Morgan was lying on her back with her arm across her face. She turned when Melanie walked in the room.

"My back hurts," she said in a half-crying, pitiful voice.

"I'm sorry. Can I get you some Tylenol?"

"Already took two pills about thirty minutes ago, but it hasn't eased off any. Mama, will you massage my back? Maybe that will help."

"Sure."

Morgan turned on her side. Melanie sat on the floor next to the couch and began to slowly but firmly massage Morgan's aching back. For a few minutes, neither of them spoke.

"Mama, I have been looking in the baby name book, but I still think I will name the baby Noah if it is a boy."

"Noah." Melanie repeated. "I've liked that name since the first time you told me. I don't know any Noahs, so that is good. A new name for a new little life."

"If it is a girl, I think I will name her Leah."

"I like that, too. What happened to Crystal?" Melanie asked, smiling.

"I decided I like Leah better."

"Me, too," Melanie agreed.

"The ultrasound shows it's most likely a boy, but they weren't a hundred percent sure. Oh—Donna wants to give me a baby shower. I know we can't invite everyone like we would if I was married and having a white man's baby."

Melanie shrugged. Unfortunately, Morgan was telling the truth and she was glad she was mature enough to accept the facts and consequences.

"That will be great. We can have it here, and I can help with the expenses."

"Thanks, Mama. I will tell Donna and get her to call you."

"Okay. Now, does your back feel any better?"

"Yeah, it does."

"Good, because now I have to go cook dinner."

"What are you cooking?"

"Stuffed peppers okay?"

Morgan smiled. It was her favorite.

"Take a nap; it'll be a while."

"Sounds good to me." Morgan turned her back, adjusted her pillow, and got as comfortable as her awkward body would allow.

Melanie headed upstairs to change before going to the kitchen. There was a message blinking on the answering machine. She hoped it was Ron. It was—just a hello message and a request to call him later. Melanie smiled. She would definitely call him after dinner. Melanie had not told Ron about the baby's father yet. She was waiting to get to know him better before sharing details of Morgan's pregnancy. A lot of people still had a problem with interracial relationships, and he might be one of those people, judging by some of the comments he had made. She hoped not. She was beginning to fall in love with him, and she knew he was falling in love with her. She wanted it to work.

Later on that night, Melanie called Ron back to chat. He was such a nice, easy-going person. Melanie enjoyed talking to him and found herself comfortable talking about most anything. Still, she had not been able to find the courage to talk to him about Morgan's pregnancy. Melanie knew she would have to do it soon before someone else told him. She preferred it come from her. Ron asked her out for Friday night. Of course, she said yes.

The next day at work, Melanie was in her office and heard two people arguing. She stepped out into the hall and listened more closely. It sounded like it was coming from Tawanna's room. As she walked towards the room, she could tell it was Tawanna's father raising his voice.

"Don't you be telling any lies to these people. Do you hear me, girl? No lies!"

Melanie stepped up to the door to investigate the commotion. Mr. Carter looked startled for a second. Tawanna stared at her father, her eyes wild and full of hate, but said nothing.

"What's going on?" Melanie inquired.

"Nothing. We're just having a family discussion," Mr. Carter said, irritated. He was not happy about the interruption.

Melanie didn't care. "Tawanna, are you okay?

For a moment the girl did not reply.

"Tawanna?"

"Yes, ma'am."

"If you need me, I will be in my office just down the hall. Call if you need anything."

"Yes, ma'am."

Mr. Carter shrugged his shoulders. "What? I'm not allowed to talk to my daughter?"

"Sure, Mr. Carter. As long as you don't abuse her."

Tawanna's head jerked up, and for a brief moment, her eyes locked onto Melanie's. Melanie turned and walked out. She thought about the look in Tawanna's eyes and wondered what that was all about. What had she said? "As long as you don't abuse her."

Tawanna looked like a deer caught in headlights. Melanie scratched her head. What was she hiding? Did her father know something he wasn't telling? Is that why he was so angry with her? Had he abused her? Hit her? What? Sooner or later, it would have to come out, or that poor girl would never be at peace.

Speaking of secrets, Melanie's mind drifted to Morgan and her pregnancy. She had to tell Ron about Morgan and wondered if it would make any difference in their relationship. She prayed it would not. It shouldn't, but then again, men in this area really had a lot of prejudices against white girls dating black guys. It was like they felt their territory had been invaded. They absolutely hated it.

As things began to get busy, Melanie forgot the puzzling eye contact with Tawanna. She had so many things on her mind. When Dr. Williams came in, he sent Melanie to get her. Dr. Williams, Tawanna, and Melanie met in the conference room for another session. Tawanna's wrist was beginning to heal, but her soul was not.

Dr. Williams began by saying, "Tawanna, you would make my life much easier if you would confide in me. I am your friend, and I am here to help you."

Tawanna looked away as usual, tears in her sad brown eyes.

"I have to know what you plan to do about the baby. If you plan to give it up, we must make plans for an adoption agency to get involved." Dr. Williams leaned over and took Tawanna's hand. He patted the top of it. Slowly, she pulled it back. Dr. Williams leaned back in his chair, puzzled. It was like she couldn't stand to be touched, even though he meant no harm.

"Tawanna? You have to talk to me."

Tawanna turned and looked into Dr. Williams' eyes. "I hate this baby. I don't want a baby, especially not this baby."

"Okay, then we need to talk to your parents and let them know your decision."

"No!" Tawanna burst into tears. "This is my decision, not theirs."

"You're right, sweetie; it is your decision. However, I feel you need the support of your family."

"Support? I have no support."

"Sure you do, they love you."

"Yeah—too much." Tawanna had a strange look on her face.

Again, Dr. Williams felt there was something he was supposed to be reading between the lines. Why didn't she just come out and tell him what she was hiding? Melanie, too, was confused by Tawanna's coldness towards her parents. She knew teenagers had differences with their parents, but Tawanna's seemed more that just some teenage drama.

Dr. Williams stood up. "Okay, Tawanna, I will call the adoption agency, and they will come and talk to you this week. I want you to be sure this is what you want. Because you are a minor, I have to discuss this with your parents."

Tawanna shrugged her shoulders. "Whatever." She stared out the window in silence.

"Tawanna, I will talk to you again tomorrow; by that time, I will have spoken to your parents about your wish to give the baby up for adoption."

Tawanna never flinched. "Good. The sooner this baby is out of my body, the better I will like it. I will never have a life as long as I have to be reminded of—" She stopped, never taking her eyes from the window.

"Reminded of what?" coaxed Dr. Williams.

"Hell," she answered, barely loud enough for Dr. Williams to hear. Tawanna got up and walked out of the room, pulling the door closed behind her.

Dr. Williams thought adoption probably was the best solution. If she hated the baby that much, it would be better off, but Tawanna's parents would probably not be happy about the decision.

They were very prominent in the community, and it would probably be embarrassing for the family. Nevertheless, Tawanna's feelings should be the deciding factor. He would talk to them later today and help them with the adoption proceeding, should it come to that. He felt it was a strong possibility.

Dr. Williams sat there a moment, and it was like a light bulb went on in his head. Melanie was watching him, and she knew that look.

"What is it, Dr. Williams? You look as if you just hit the jackpot."

"Better than that, sweetheart. I just figured out why she hates the baby. It is so clear. Why didn't we see it sooner?"

"What, Dr. Williams?" Melanie asked, confused.

"Melanie, it is so obvious. Tawanna was raped!"

"What? How do you know?"

"It all adds up," he continued. "Why else would she hate the baby so much? If she loved a boy enough to let him have sex with her, she would not despise the baby the way she does. She mentioned something about being in hell or living in hell, or something about hell. Yes, that's it! My God, that poor child. She was raped."

Now that it was sinking in, Dr. Williams looked compassionate. He brushed both hands through his hair and threw his arms up as he paced the room. "What took me so long to figure it out? She gave us all the hints." Dr. Williams shook his head, disgusted with himself.

"Dr. Williams, that doesn't make any sense. If she were raped, she would have reported it to the police."

"There could be several reasons she didn't report it."

"Such as? Who wouldn't report a rape?" Melanie asked, staring at Dr. Williams.

"Melanie, you would be surprised at the number of rapes that go unreported."

"Really?" she asked, finding that hard to believe.

"Hundreds, no thousands, every year, go unreported, and the rapists go free to do it again and again."

"Why? Why would anybody let someone get away with rape?"

"Pride, shame, feeling as if they may, in some way, be the blame. Fear for their reputation and even for their life. There are lots of reasons they don't report it. Tomorrow, I will find a way to bring the subject of rape up and see what kind of response I get. I can't just ask her; obviously, if she hasn't reported it to the police, she is not just going to tell me about it."

"I guess you're right," Melanie agreed.

"I have a feeling she is dying to tell the truth, but she doesn't want to be the one to open a bad can of worms. She knows rape is a serious crime, and whoever did this to her will spend a long time in jail."

"Which is where he needs to be!" fired Melanie.

"Of course he does, but she, for whatever reason, doesn't want to be the one to put him there."

"Dr. Williams, you're beginning to sound like Perry Mason trying to solve a murder mystery."

"Well, it is definitely a mystery, and I am trying to solve it," Dr. Williams agreed.

"Good luck on this one. I have a feeling you're going to need it."

"I think you're right, sweetheart."

"Well, it's another un-boring day at Eastside," Melanie teased.

Dr. Williams stood up, stretching his tall, stiff body. "I swear I'm getting old. I can't sit thirty minutes without feeling like I can barely move my body."

"Dr. Williams, people like you never get old; they just fade away into the sunset."

Dr. Williams grinned and put his arm around Melanie's shoulder as they walked out into the hall. "I guess you're right, or at least, I like to think you are. And if I do just fade away into the sunset, please let it be somewhere like Hawaii, sipping on a Long Island ice tea, watching hula girls dancing in the sunset, and not here at Eastside." He laughed and gave Melanie a little squeeze. "See ya next time."

Dr. Williams was so likeable. All the nurses loved him, and they enjoyed when he came into the facility. He always had them laughing about something. Most thought he was sexy for his age. Best of all, they all respected him. He was a caring, compassionate doctor. Melanie thought about that as she watched him walk out the door. She was confidant he could help Tawanna. He would stop at nothing to free her from her miseries.

It was five o'clock, and another exciting day had come and gone at work. That's what Melanie liked about her job; it was never boring. Today she had admitted a lady in her eighties that had become combative at home and hit her husband. The husband had been in tears while trying to do the paperwork for her admission. Melanie's heart had gone out to him. He told her they had been married over sixty years, had nine children together, and lost two to cancer and one to alcoholism. It had not been an easy life, but through it all they had loved each other unconditionally. That's why it had hurt him so badly when she hit him. "Not the physical pain," he said in tears. "I know she would never hurt me. She is just not herself these days. I don't know what to do anymore."

His son arrived about then and helped his dad finish the paperwork. Melanie was glad to see family there for moral support. It was going to be a tough road as the doctors looked for the answers to his wife's mental changes. It could be a number of things, and Melanie couldn't even begin to guess at this point what was going on with his wife. She just knew she felt sorry for him because he was suffering for his inability to help the woman he loved more than anything in the world. If she ever found a true love like that, she would grab it and hold it forever. She thought of Ron. Tonight she would talk with him about Morgan, the baby, and the father.

Chapter Fourteen

*W*hen Melanie got home, Morgan was upstairs, as usual. She didn't go out very much these days. She felt sick a lot, as well as tired and sleepy. All the symptoms of pregnancy. Hey, nobody said it was fun. Should have thought about that, Melanie thought sarcastically.

Melanie had planned a little romantic dinner for Ron and herself. She would feed Morgan before he got there. She wanted them to have some time alone to talk about things that were on her mind and felt it best for Morgan not to be around, since most of it was about her and the baby. Also, she didn't know how he would take the news. Melanie hated herself for feeling as if she had to apologize or explain Morgan's pregnancy to Ron, or to anyone else, for that matter. She especially hated herself for feeling she had to apologize that the baby's daddy was black. She felt like each time she told someone, she was apologizing for it. It was like she was ashamed of the baby. She was not. But it did come out like that every time. She hated that and made up her mind not to let it be that way any more. From now on, she would state the facts with no apologies or excuses.

The door bell rang promptly at seven, and Melanie took a deep breath. She hoped she looked pretty in her sexy black dress and sandals. She had on red lipstick and her blonde, shoulder-length hair softly hung around her face. She had put on just a touch of the perfume that he had given her for Christmas.

When she opened the door, it was obvious he liked what he saw. He smiled and gave her a kiss on the cheek and then softly on the mouth. He put his hands on her waist and pushed her back to look at her, and he smiled again. "You look great," he said.

"Thank you kindly, sir. So do you," she teased, admiring his taste in clothes. She thought he looked sharp in his khaki pants and burgundy shirt. She took his hand as they walked in. "How was your day?"

"Oh about as boring as usual in the day of a salesman," he replied. "And yours?" he asked.

"As un- boring as you can imagine in the day of a psych hospital," she said truthfully. She never discussed her patients with anyone, so that was the extent of her comment.

"I can only imagine," Ron answered, raising his eyebrows.

Melanie led Ron to the dining room. Candles were burning throughout the house.

"What's the occasion?" Ron asked.

"No occasion—just dinner for two."

"Oh. I like the sound of that," Ron said, grinning.

"So do I. That's why I planned it that way," she said softly, her eyes meeting his.

He smiled, exposing a boyish grin.

Even with all the flirting going on—and she was flirting—he noticed a bit of nervousness. He couldn't quite make it out. The dinner, the candles, the wine? What was the occasion? Had he forgotten something? He pulled out the chair for her and poured her a glass of wine and then a glass for himself.

"I would like to make a toast," he said. "If you don't mind."

"Sure," she answered, smiling at him. What a nice guy he was, and he was nice looking, too. He was tall, about six feet and two hundred and twenty pounds. His blondish hair was thinning on top, and he looked distinguished. Ron picked up his glass, and so did Melanie. They held the glasses in the air as Ron began his toast.

"To my hostess, thank you for making this evening so special, for whatever reason. You are a very special lady, with or without the dinner, the candles, or the wine, and I hope I will have the honor of many, many more dinners with you, whether it is by candlelight or daylight or moonlight." He moved his glass towards hers, and they clinked as they touched.

They both took a sip of the wine. Their eyes met and held for a brief second before she looked away, afraid he might see she was falling in love with him.

Dinner was very romantic, just as she had planned, but she knew what lay ahead. After their meal, she asked him to sit in the den. It was a little cool, so she lit the fireplace, and they snuggled up together on the couch looking into the warm glow of the fire. Melanie cleared her throat, as she did sometimes when she was nervous. Ron sensed something had been on her mind the entire night, but he waited patiently until she was ready to tell him what it was.

"Ron, there is something I need to talk to you about. I am not apologizing for it; I am just letting you know. Melanie cleared her throat again.

Ron looked at her, waiting. "What is it, Melanie? I know you're not pregnant," he laughed, trying to ease her tension.

"No, I'm not, but Morgan is," she said, looking down at her hands.

"Yes, I know; you told me already."

She had told him Morgan was pregnant, but he had never asked about the father. He had to know before someone else told him.

"Sweetheart, I can tell you are really bothered by it, but surely you don't think it will be a problem for us. I mean, I'm sorry and all that, but she is not the first young girl to get pregnant and not be married, and she won't be the last." Ron took her hands in his. "Look, I don't mean to make light of this because I know it hurts you to see her put this burden on herself, but she'll get through it and so will you. I will be here for you, and for her, too." Ron kissed her lightly on the cheek and pulled her into his chest, closing his arms around her as if to protect her.

After a moment, Melanie pulled back. She looked at Ron, a tear running down her cheek. "Ron, there's more. Being pregnant is only half the problem; the other half is the father," she said sadly.

"Do you know him? Is he not willing to stand up and take responsibility for his own child?" he asked, raising his voice a little.

"No, I don't know him. Morgan has told me very little about him except—" Melanie paused.

"What?" Ron asked hesitantly.

"He is black," Melanie blurted as her voice cracked.

Melanie watched Ron's reaction carefully through tear-filled eyes. It surprised him and even though he tried not to react, she could tell it shook him. For a moment, neither spoke. Melanie got up, walked over to the fireplace, and warmed her hands. She suddenly felt chilled; plus, she wanted to have her back to Ron while he let it sink in a little, just in case it made him uncomfortable, which she knew it did.

Slowly she turned and folded her arms as if to keep the chill off, but mostly it was to keep from shaking. Why was she so nervous? It really had nothing to do with him. He didn't have to raise the baby. He didn't have to bear shame. He didn't have to do anything. Regardless, it could make a difference in their relationship.

Ron got off the couch, came over, and put his arms around her. "I'm sorry, Melanie. I know this makes it more complicated."

Melanie didn't deny that. She let him embrace her and comfort her. After a few moments of just holding her close, saying nothing, he lifted her chin and kissed her softly on the lips.

"I'm here for you," he said softly.

Her tear-streaked face lay on his chest as he held her. After a few moments, he led her back to the couch where they again cuddled up in front of the fire. She closed her eyes as she lay in his arms. For this moment, she felt safe and content. Everything was going to be okay. With the warmth of the fire and the closeness of his body, she drifted off to sleep. The peace was welcome. Ron let her sleep and watched her breathe softly. After about an hour, he nudged her gently.

"Hey, sleepyhead, better get up to bed. I gotta go home. Tomorrow is a work day," he said, smiling at her.

Melanie was surprised she had fallen asleep. She hadn't been sleeping well lately. She had been worried about several things, including Morgan, the arrival of the new baby, Ron's reaction, as well as everyone else's, and of course, her son and his declining condition. Suddenly, Melanie remembered the earlier conversation and looked at his face to see if she could tell what he was thinking. Nothing looked any different. He didn't act any different. Maybe it didn't make any difference after all. Well, at least the secret was out. She would deal with the consequences, whatever they may be. She couldn't keep it secret forever.

Melanie walked Ron to the door. He again took her in his arms and hugged her. "I will call you tomorrow," he said, as he bent down and kissed her lightly on the lips.

Melanie smiled up at him. "I surely hope so."

"I will," he promised, squeezing her hand.

He turned and walked out the door. She leaned against the door after she locked it behind him, thinking about how the night had gone. She really didn't know what she had expected him to do, or how she expected him to react. What could he do? It wasn't his daughter.

The next day, Ron called to say hello, but he never mentioned the night before or what they had discussed. She didn't know if this was a good sign or a bad sign. She assumed he would just lay low, and not say anything either way, which was probably best, especially if what he felt or thought was negative. She didn't know if she felt comfortable talking to him about her feelings and fears, since she really didn't know what his beliefs were about different races having children together. She hoped he would be okay with it because she really did need a friend to lean on right now. Besides, she liked him a lot and knew they were headed for a much deeper relationship.

Chapter Fifteen

The next few days were pretty uneventful.

On Wednesday, Dr. Williams met with Tawanna again. He felt in his heart that Tawanna had been raped, and that was why she was reacting to the pregnancy with such vengeance. He would talk to her about his suspicions in this session.

When Tawanna came into the meeting room, she still wore the look of shame, disgust, and sadness. Dr. William's heart went out to her. Leona came in and sat at the table with Dr. Williams to get him to sign some papers before he started his session. She was making small talk about her headaches and occasional flashes of light in her vision while Dr. Williams grunted and rubbed his chin.

"It sounds like you need to go see your doctor. Don't wait," he said, concerned.

"Exactly what I told her," interrupted Melanie.

"It could be a number of things, from migraines to something more serious," he said. "Either way, you should be checked out. You should have already been to a doctor."

"I'm seeing one now," grinned Leona.

"I'm a psychiatrist, not the kind of doctor you need," he responded.

"I know, I know," she answered. "But you know how we medical people are. We doctor everybody but ourselves," Leona laughed. "No reflection on you, of course," she added.

"Yes, I know how medical people are," he mocked. "Seriously, make an appointment, Leona; it's nothing to kid around about."

"That is exactly what I am going to do as soon as I get a chance," she answered, more seriously this time.

"Well, like I said; don't wait."

Leona nodded. "Okay, you're the doctor."

"And don't forget it," he said out the corner of his mouth.

"I told you so," Melanie grunted, "but don't listen to me. Nobody else does."

Leona stuck her tongue out at Melanie as she left the room. Melanie returned the favor.

Dr. Williams shook his head. "You're both so professional," he said, grinning.

Dr. Williams turned and looked at Tawanna. She was ignoring all of them and seemed totally uninterested in their conversation. Dr. Williams' demeanor turned serious. "Tawanna, have you thought about the adoption of your baby and if that is truly what you want to do?"

"Yes, I have, and yes, it is," she answered coldly.

"Then we must include your parents in the arrangements, since you are underage."

"Fine." She looked at Dr. Williams, her eyes boring into him.

He didn't know which was worse—when she wouldn't look at him or when she stared him down.

"Tawanna, I want to talk to you about your pregnancy. It seems you are more than just upset about it."

She continued to stare at him, never flinching, almost as if she were trying to prove something. "What's your point, Doctor?"

"I think maybe you were raped."

Her eyes widened, as if she couldn't believe he had said that. "Raped?"

"It makes sense. That is why you are so angry. If you were pregnant by a boyfriend that cared about you, you wouldn't be this devastated."

Dr. Williams carefully watched Tawanna's body language. Body language told more than words sometimes. He had definitely hit a nerve.

"And what would you call rape?" she sneered.

"Rape," Dr. Williams started softly, "is sexual intercourse or attempted intercourse without consent. Rape involves all forms of sexual victimization," he said compassionately, knowing it would have been a very traumatic experience for her. "In your case, it would be statutory rape because you are under the age of eighteen." He definitely had her attention. She was listening and taking it all in. "Do your parents know?" he asked gently.

"I never said I was raped," she said sharply.

"You didn't say you weren't, either," he came back easily. "Tawanna, please let us help you. If you were raped, do you want the bastard to go free and do it again? More than fifty percent of rape victims are between the ages of fifteen and nineteen. Think about some other young girl going through what you're going through. You can bet he will do it again and again, as long as he gets away with it." Dr. Williams paused a moment, letting Tawanna absorb the information. "We need to tell your parents."

"No," she screamed and jumped up, flipping the chair over.

Melanie jumped at the sudden outburst.

"No! No! No!" she fired again, louder each time.

"Tawanna, you cannot go through this alone. Even if you give the baby up for adoption, you need your parents' help."

"Dr. Williams, you listen to me." Her brown eyes flashed. "I will commit suicide before I ask for their help."

Obviously her home life was not what he thought it was, or she would have welcomed their support. "Okay, I will respect your requests not to tell them, even though I think you should."

"And who made you God?" she snapped. "And where was He when I cried out for his help? 'Oh, God, please help me,' I prayed the whole time it was happening. 'Please, God. Please.' A child crying for her God that never came to help. Where was God when I needed him? Where was God when I begged to die?" Tawanna's defenses broke, and she began to weep hysterically. "Answer me! Where was God? How and why did He let this happen to me? Why? Was I such a bad person that I deserved to be treated this way? Did I deserve to be hurt over and over again? What did I do to be humiliated this way? You want to know what I think of God now? There is no God," she finished, still crying.

Bingo! She was raped. He hurt for the pain she was in, but this outburst was the beginning to her healing. He let her continue.

"I tried to resist, but he forced himself on me. I begged him to stop, but he wouldn't," she cried.

Melanie put her hand on Tawanna's arm.

Dr. Williams said nothing. If he spoke, she might stop, and he wanted her to vent.

"I was only ten the first time he approached me," she said tearfully.

She was wiping tears as she talked. Melanie handed her tissues with her free hand, keeping her other hand on Tawanna's arm. She patted gently. Her heart was breaking for the girl.

"I was frightened and started to cry," she went on. "He told me he loved me and if I told anyone, he would get in trouble."

Now Dr. Williams knew her abuser was a relative or a friend of the family.

"He told me I would have to go live in a foster home if I told on him because he would be sent away and my mother would hate me."

Dr. Williams sat up and looked at Tawanna in disbelief. "Tawanna, your father abused you?"

Tawanna stopped, surprised at her own admissions. She didn't know what to say, but it was already out of the bag. It was too late to back up now, and they all knew it. She started to cry helplessly, and her shoulders jerked with sobs.

Melanie moved her chair closer and put her arms around her. "Let it out, sweetie," she said, feeling a motherly protectiveness. "You just go ahead and cry. You have good reason to cry. Let it all out."

Tawanna couldn't speak for a few minutes as she wept.

Dr. Williams was in shock. He'd had no idea the abuser was Tawanna's father. He was a prominent figure in town. You just never knew what went on behind closed doors. He waited for Tawanna to gain some composure before urging her to continue. "Sweetheart, does your mother know about this? Does anyone know about this?"

"No," she answered between sniffles. "I don't think she ever thought he would do such a thing to his own child." She looked at Dr. Williams, sadly this time, with questions in her eyes. "What would make a father do that?" she asked pathetically.

"Honey, I have no idea. It certainly is a sickness, but I can't explain it or understand it. Maybe things happened to him in his childhood. I just don't know," Dr. Williams said, shaking his head. "Does your father know the baby is his?"

"Yes, he knows I have not had a boy in that way. I hate sex, and I can't stand to be touched by a man," she said.

Dr. Williams knew she would need a lot of counseling in the future. Dr. Williams' head was spinning with questions and thoughts. What to do now? He did not want to overwhelm Tawanna or frighten her worse than she was already. Her father had to be reported to the authorities, and he had to report this to Child Protective Services. What a mess—even more so than he had feared. He now understood why she was so devastated about the pregnancy—and with good reason. Dr. Williams was now also worried about the pregnancy for many more reasons. He wished she had opted for an abortion, but it was too late for that now. She was too far along.

"Please, Dr. Williams, you can't tell anyone," she pleaded.

He looked at her sympathetically. "Tawanna, I have to tell the authorities. By law, I have to report this."

Tawanna began to cry again. "My life is ruined, and so is my mother's and my brother's. It's my fault."

It was not her fault. He took her by the shoulders and stared into her young eyes. "Tawanna, don't ever say that. You are the victim. You did nothing wrong. Your father took advantage of a child. His own child. There is no excuse for his actions."

Tawanna's lips trembled.

"You are a good person, and you must not let this destroy your life. We are here to help you. You are not alone. Do you hear me, sweetheart? We are going to be here all the way for you."

Tawanna leaned towards Dr. Williams as if exhausted. Dr. Williams gently put his arms around her, not wanting to make her uncomfortable, but wanting to comfort her. She was trembling all over. He held her until she stopped shaking. Tawanna seemed to welcome the support. After a few moments, Dr. Williams asked Melanie if she would sit with Tawanna until she felt better. He was worried about her emotional health as well as her physical health. He suggested she lay down for a while and try to relax. Melanie walked with her to her room, her arm around her shoulder. She, too, had been shocked by Mr. Carter's actions. He'd always seemed like a good father and husband when she saw them in public.

Dr. Williams stepped out of the facility, lit a cigarette, and took a deep puff, something he rarely did anymore, but he did keep a pack in his briefcase for times like this. Everyone knew something was worrying him when they saw him smoking. They were right this time. About the time he lit the cigarette, he saw Sidney Carter step out of his car. Dr. Williams grew enraged as he watched the sophisticated gentleman walk towards him. Mr. Carter had a smile on his face as he stuck out his hand for a shake.

Dr. Williams took his hand and squeezed it so hard he almost broke it. "You lousy son of a bitch," Dr. Williams said, angry.

Mr. Carter looked shocked, and Dr. Williams saw the fear in his eyes.

"You ought to be put under the jail," Dr. Williams snarled.

Sidney Carter tried to regain his composure and pull his hand back from the excruciating grip Dr. Williams had on it. "I don't know what in the hell you are talking about," he said, sounding confused.

"The hell you don't, you child molester!" Dr. Williams said, inflamed.

Sidney Carter stared at him, his face turning pale.

"I will personally see that you rot in jail for what you did to that poor child," he promised. Dr. Williams was angrier than he had ever been in his sixty-two years. His heart was pounding and the vessel in his neck looked like it was about to explode.

Mr. Carter stared at him, speechless. He was afraid to say anything, afraid Dr. Williams would punch him.

"I will be in touch with the authorities," Dr. Williams said, "and you will pay for what you put Tawanna through. What were you thinking, man? Have you no love for your daughter? If any other man had done this to her, you would be ready to kill the SOB. Your wife is going to find out, the community is going to find out, and you will lose your job, your home, and your family." Dr. Williams was furious and let go of Carter's hand, holding him in his stare.

About that time, Melanie burst through the hospital door, "Dr. Williams, thank God you're still here. It's Tawanna; come quickly, something's wrong!"

Dr. Williams started to run back into the hospital, and so did Mr. Carter. Dr. Williams turned abruptly. "Not you! Get out of my hospital."

Carter stopped in his tracks, knowing if he took one more step, Dr. Williams would probably attack him.

Dr. Williams ran to Tawanna's room. She was crouched over, holding her stomach and crying. "The cramps are so bad I can hardly breathe," Tawanna cried. "What's happening to me?"

"Tawanna, try to calm down and breathe slowly," answered Dr. Williams. "See if you can lie down on your bed, sweetie."

Dr. Williams and Melanie helped her to the bed, and she lay down, curling up in a fetal position, still holding her stomach. Dr. Williams saw several large spots of bright red blood on her jeans.

"Melanie, call 911; we need to get her to the hospital, fast. Call her mother and tell her to meet us at the hospital."

Dr. Williams wanted her there in case he needed her to sign any emergency papers; plus, having her mother near would help calm Tawanna.

Tawanna was rocking slowly back and forth on her bed, crouched in a fetal position. "Please, God, don't let me die. I don't want to die," she cried. Tawanna took hold of Dr. Williams' arm, "Please, Dr. Williams, don't let me die."

Tears streamed down her young face. She looked so young, just like a child. Briefly, he thought of Carter and felt his heart rate quicken.

She was losing a lot of blood fast.

"Where's the damn rescue?" he yelled.

"They're coming now," Melanie assured him.

The rescue team started working on her immediately, taking her vitals and starting an IV.

Dr. Williams felt a knot in his stomach. She was still losing blood and crying softly.

"Oh, God, what else are you going to do to me? Why do you hate me so much? What did I do? God, please forgive me for whatever I did that made you hate me," she prayed. "God, it's not my fault; I was innocent, and even though I prayed, you turned your back on me."

Dr. Williams still held her hand. He could hardly stand to hear her pleas. It tore his insides up listening to her.

"God, I prayed to you. And they that know thy name will put their trust in thee; for thou, Lord, hast not forsaken them that seek thee." (Psalm 9:10) Every time he hurt me, I prayed over and over, and it happened again and again, week after week, month after month for four years. God, I loved you so much, and I thought you loved me. God, you did forsake me. Why did you turn your back on me? I don't understand."

It was like no one else was around. Tawanna was having a conversation with God, almost unaware of the bleeding and the rescue team working on her. Slowly, Tawanna's head fell to the side, and she went limp. Her tight grip on Dr. Williams' hand dropped, and so did his heart. He looked at the paramedics. She was still breathing, but it was faint.

"She passed out from the blood loss," one team member said as they prepared to move her to the trauma unit at the hospital. Doctors were waiting there to do whatever they could to save her life.

Dr. Williams walked with them to the transport outside. "I will meet you at the hospital."

The transport moved out, turning on lights and sirens. Dr. Williams was worried she might not make it. He went back in to call her mother. Mrs. Carter answered the phone, and Dr. Williams told her Tawanna was likely losing the baby and had lost a lot of blood. Mrs. Carter started to cry.

"Mrs. Carter, please calm down and get to the hospital immediately."

"I am on my way," she said through her sobs. "I'll call her father."

Dr. Williams shuddered. "He already knows. He was at the hospital when she got sick," he said, trying not to show his anger. "I'll meet you there," he said, almost gritting his teeth at the thought of Sidney Carter.

He slammed the phone down so hard everyone could hear it down the hall. He was getting riled up again.

Melanie walked over and put her arm on his. "Are you okay?"

Dr. Williams hesitated. "Not really," he answered honestly, "but I'll survive." Deep down in his heart, he thought Tawanna was better off losing the child, but he also knew she would have to bear the burden of feeling she had caused that, too—if she survived herself, he thought sadly. He was not at all sure she would.

When Melanie got home, she could not help but think of Tawanna and hope she would be okay. She was pretty sure she had lost the baby. Just like Dr. Williams, she had mixed feelings. She knew it was probably the best for all concerned. Morgan walked into the kitchen, interrupting her thoughts, and she glanced at Morgan's stomach. Melanie was thankful it was not Morgan in the hospital having a miscarriage.

"Mom, is something wrong? You look worried."

Melanie told Morgan that something had happened at work, and Morgan knew not to ask any more questions. She knew her mother respected the patients' rights to privacy. Melanie didn't want to worry Morgan about a possible miscarriage. Morgan was six months along, and her nerves were already on edge.

"Well, I had an interesting day at work," Morgan said, shifting the subject.

Melanie looked at her, waiting. "Oh?"

"Oh, yeah," Morgan said, dragging it out.

"What, Morgan? Are you going to tell me, or just let me guess all day? When you work for your aunt, how hard can it be?" Melanie laughed.

"Did you say I work for my aunt?"

"Yes, Morgan, your aunt."

"In a Christian book store?" Morgan asked, emphasizing the word "Christian" strongly.

"Yes!" Melanie said impatiently.

"Not anymore," Morgan said, her eyes wide open, as if to make a statement.

"What are you talking about?"

"I got fired today."

"Fired?" Melanie asked, surprised.

"F-I-R-E-D," Morgan spelled out.

Melanie sat down on the bar stool, trying to make sense of what Morgan had told her.

Morgan threw her hands up. "You heard me right. Fired."

Melanie couldn't believe her ears. "Your Aunt Jenny fired you?"

"Just a little while ago, in fact."

"Morgan, why? What did you do?"

"I got pregnant!" Morgan answered quickly.

"Pregnant?"

"That's what she said," Morgan replied.

"What did she say?" Melanie felt the heat rising to her face.

"Aunt Jenny said, and I quote," Morgan started. "'Morgan, I need to talk to you about something.' 'Okay,' I said. She came over, put her arm around me, and said, 'Honey, I think it's best if you stop working here. You're beginning to show, and we don't want people talking.'"

Melanie's mouth dropped. "You're kidding me," she said when she found her voice. Her face was crimson, and her heart was pounding.

Morgan continued, "Then Aunt Jenny said, 'There's no hard feelings, sweetheart; everybody makes mistakes, but we have to protect our business, and this is bad for business. Then she rubbed my belly." Morgan imitated her aunt rubbing her belly. "Well, from what I understand, God doesn't make mistakes, so if there is a baby inside this belly, and God created that baby, it's not a mistake," Morgan stated.

Melanie didn't know how to argue with that. It was true that God didn't make mistakes, and he was the only one that could put life into a woman's womb, and the only one that could create the miracle of birth. Morgan was right about that. Melanie felt sorry for her. She was putting on a smile, but she knew Morgan well enough to know her feelings were hurt. Even as a child, Morgan would try to make something funny out of something that really hurt her. Melanie didn't know what to say.

"It doesn't matter," Morgan said, shrugging her shoulders.

"Did she mention the father?" Melanie asked curiously.

"Actually, she did not," Morgan answered.

"I'm surprised," Melanie said sarcastically. "I'm going to talk to her tomorrow."

"Mama, no! I don't want to be where I'm not wanted," Morgan said.

Melanie could relate to that, and Morgan was right. It would only make matters worse.

"Well, I think it's crummy when your own family turns its back on you, especially those that claim to be Christians. If that is Christian, I don't want to be one," Melanie said harshly. "Honey, I'm sorry, but this is just the beginning. I wish I were wrong, and everybody accepted the baby with open arms, but that's not going to happen. This is what it is like in the real world, and you have to get tough if you are going to get through this."

"I know it's going to be hard, Mama. I never thought it would be easy, but I confess I was surprised today when Aunt Jenny told me not to come back." Her eyes filled with tears. "If I were her daughter instead of her niece, would she stand by me or desert me?"

"I expect she would stand by you if she is the mother I think she is," Melanie answered.

"But she didn't stand by me," Morgan said.

"It's different when it's your own child," Melanie said.

"Why?"

"Trust me, honey; it just is. You'll soon find out that nothing will come between you and your child," Melanie said, patting Morgan's stomach.

"I already know that, or I would have had an abortion like everyone wanted me to," Morgan said coolly.

Melanie nodded.

"I guess it's a good thing I have you for my mama instead of Aunt Jenny."

"I guess so," Melanie said, smiling.

"I'm tired; I'm going lie down a while before supper," Morgan said.

Melanie watched Morgan walk out of the room. Her Aunt Jenny would not be the last of the rejections. There would be many more to come.

As Melanie fixed supper, she thought of Ron. He had been a little distant towards Morgan since she had talked to him about the pregnancy. She didn't think it was the pregnancy, as much as the father being black. She couldn't swear that was it, but she had seen the expression on his face when she told him. He had tried to hide the surprise, but she had caught the look of disapproval just before he looked away. Once he got over the initial shock and realized she was watching his response, he came over and put his arms around her to comfort her, but said nothing. She could only wonder what was going through his mind and if it would affect their relationship somehow.

In a few minutes, Morgan came back downstairs, and sat down with a thump to eat with her mother. "Mama, I feel like a blimp already, and I have three more months to go."

"You are not a blimp. You are pregnant, and unfortunately, gaining weight goes with having a baby. I hate to tell you, kiddo, but the worst is yet to come."

Morgan frowned.

Melanie grinned and patted her on the head. "So, would you like to back out now?"

"Like that is an option," Morgan sighed.

"I was just wondering if you would if you could."

"No, Mama, I wouldn't. I want this baby."

"I know."

Melanie gave Morgan a look of compassion and understanding. Only a mother could understand the joy of giving birth. Morgan truly wanted this baby. Melanie leaned over and hugged her. "You will be a good mama. That little baby will be blessed to have you for its mommy."

Morgan wrapped her arms around Melanie and leaned her head on her shoulder. For a moment, they just sat there holding on to each other—mother and daughter.

Melanie felt so much love for Morgan and her unborn grandchild. She knew Morgan was strong willed and smart enough to deal with other people's rudeness and ignorance. She hugged Morgan a little tighter at the thought of people mistreating her. She would be there to help her through the hard times and would stand beside her as long as she had breath in her body.

After a few minutes, Morgan told Melanie she was going upstairs to read for a while. Melanie kissed Morgan on the head.

"I love you, Punky Wunky."

Morgan smiled at the nickname and had a flashback of one Valentine's when she was in the eighth grade, and her mama sent flowers to the school on Valentine's Day. On the outside of card was Morgan Hutchings, but on the inside was "You will always be our Punky Wunky. Love, Mama and Daddy."

Morgan didn't show the card to the other girls and let them think the flowers were from some guy. Her mama always seemed to know what she needed. At that time, the other girls were dating, and she still was not allowed to date, so it really made her day. Morgan smiled again, remembering how jealous the other girls were that she had gotten roses from an admirer.

Ron called just as Melanie stepped out of the shower. She was glad to hear his voice. He brightened her spirits every time she talked to him. She was glad he had come into her life. They made a date for Friday night and she felt a little more at ease that everything was going to work out for them. He sounded happy to speak to her and talked for thirty minutes about his work and kids and a movie he wanted them to see, but he didn't mention Morgan or ask how she was doing. Oh, well, she thought, he probably just forgot about it. Besides he didn't have to ask about her every time they talked, did he? Of course not. She was over–reacting. He's perfectly happy with us. He called, didn't he? He wants to come over, doesn't he? No problem then, right? Melanie drifted off to sleep dreaming about Morgan and a black guy whose face she couldn't see. They were walking holding hands; she was pregnant. Morgan was laughing so hard she was holding her stomach. He was making her laugh. Then he reached over and put his hand on her stomach, turned loose her hand, stepped in front of her, got on his knees, put his hands on her waist, and laid his head on her stomach to listen to the baby's heartbeat. Morgan rested her hands on his head, pressing it close to her stomach. He said something, and Morgan bent over and kissed him on the head. He stood up, put his arms around her, and held her close to him. She looked so happy. Melanie fell into a deep sleep, leaving the two of them alone in the dream.

Chapter Sixteen

*T*awanna had lost the baby. She was stable, and her mother was sitting in a chair by the bed, her hand lying across Tawanna and her head on the side of the bed. Tawanna was heavily sedated and sleeping. Apparently, Mrs. Carter had also drifted off to sleep.

Dr. Williams came into the room to check on them, and Mrs. Carter woke. She looked exhausted.

Dr. Williams walked up and put his hand on her shoulder. "I'm sorry," he said softly.

"I know," she replied. "Thanks for all you have done for Tawanna. Dr. Williams," she started, and then she stopped to gain her composure.

He put his hand on her shoulder.

"Dr. Williams," she started again, "I know what happened to Tawanna. She was talking while she was sedated, and it wasn't making any sense." Mrs. Carter looked at Tawanna and rubbed her arm as she talked. "After a while, I put what she was saying together. I couldn't believe it. I thought she was hallucinating or having nightmares or something. She kept saying the same thing over and over—'God, please forgive me,' 'God, why did you forsake me?' 'God, why did you let him hurt me?' 'God, he is my daddy.'" Mrs. Carter gasped and put her hand over her mouth. She stopped to gain her composure.

Dr. Williams waited patiently.

"Oh, my God! How could he?"

Dr. Williams put his hand on her arm. "I don't know," he answered, shaking his head. "I am truly sorry you had to find this out. You know I had to report him to Social Services and Child Protective Services. I had an obligation." Dr. Williams felt guilty, although he had no reason to. By law, he'd had to report it, and she knew it.

She also knew it was going to destroy her family, what Sidney Carter hadn't already destroyed. She was silent for a moment. "Yes, doctor. I understand," she said sadly. "I will tell you something you do not know."

Dr. Williams waited, wondering what else he was about to find out.

"Sidney is not Tawanna's biological father. For years, I have thought he resented her because she was not his. But God knows, I didn't know he was capable of molesting her," she said, tears in her eyes.

Dr. Williams listened, not saying anything.

"Sidney's best friend is the father. His name is Mathew Hall, and he lives in New York now. I was seventeen, and he was married with one other child. I fell in love with him. He was older, handsome, and financially well off. He loved me, too, but he could not bring himself to break up his family. When I got pregnant, he asked Sidney to marry me. I agreed because my dad was a preacher, and I was afraid of the consequences. Sidney had always liked me, and I liked him as a friend, so it seemed like a good answer to a bad situation. We managed to make a successful life together. We agreed never to tell Tawanna the truth. I felt I owed it to him not to tell her. He raised her as his own, or so I thought," she said.

"Tawanna's real father kept in touch over the years, and I sent pictures of her as she grew up. A few years ago, he approached me and wanted to tell her the truth, but I wouldn't let him. She knows him as Uncle Matt. She and I go up to New York every Christmas to shop for a few days, and while we are there, he always takes us out on the town for an evening. That is his way of being a part of her life. Tawanna likes him a lot, but she's never suspected he is her father. She's always referred to him as her favorite uncle," she said, smiling.

Dr. Williams listened sympathetically. He was still disgusted by Sidney Carter. He was still a jerk in his book.

"When Tawanna is stable and back home, I will tell her the truth. Maybe she will understand that none of this is her fault. I truly believe he resents her because she is not his, and this was his way of punishing her and me. I'm so sorry my baby had to suffer for my mistakes," she said, wiping tears from her face.

"She didn't deserve any of this. She has always been a good child," Mrs. Carter said.

"You're right; she doesn't deserve this, but now we can only try to overcome the circumstances and go on," Dr. Williams said, patting her hand. "I will be here for Tawanna and you. Tawanna will need more therapy to deal with all that has happened to her, you know."

"Yes, doctor, and I will see that she gets all the help she needs. Sidney and I are over. I already talked to him, and he has confessed everything. He begged for my forgiveness, but I can never forgive him for what he has done to Tawanna. I will never forgive him for the pain he put her through," she said stiffly.

Dr. Williams understood. He, too, would never forgive the man for what he had done to that poor girl. Tawanna stirred, and they stopped talking. Mrs. Carter leaned over and spoke to Tawanna, but she drifted back into a deep sleep. Dr. Williams hugged Lois Carter and told her he would be in later to check on Tawanna. Mrs. Carter laid her hand across Tawanna again and put her head back down on the bed beside her. She was exhausted, but she would not leave her daughter's side. She would be there when Tawanna woke up.

Chapter Seventeen

*A*s the next couple of months passed, Melanie found herself torn between her feelings for Ron and the question of whether he could truly accept her biracial grandchild—truly accept, not just put on acts of acceptance. She watched him carefully when Morgan was around. It seemed to her that something was missing in his interactions with her. Morgan was trying really hard to fit in with Ron, but he made it almost impossible for her to even carry on a conversation with him. It was almost as if he had no interest in her or chose to be distant to her. She had noticed how he reacted to other young people her age, and it was entirely different. He laughed and joked and carried on with them, but not with Morgan. He definitely treated her differently, and it was not Melanie's imagination. Ron loved her, and she felt she loved him. She really wanted someone to love and who loved her. She asked herself what it was like to be in love. She couldn't remember. She smiled as she thought of something her grandmother had told her when she was about fourteen and had just started liking boys.

Grandma remembered how she knew she was in love with Grandpa. "Eley was the only man I ever loved," she said as she reminisced. "I knew it was true love because the first time he ever held my hand, my palms got sweaty, and my faced got so flushed he asked if I was sick. I was sick all right—lovesick. For the longest time, my face would flush, I'd get sweaty palms, and my heart would race when I was near him. I knew beyond the shadow of a doubt that he was my soul mate. I can see him like it was yesterday. Her eyes twinkled at the memory. "He had the bluest eyes I'd ever seen, and he was ever so handsome. He was tall and slim, with thick, dark brown hair. He was a sight, I'll tell you that. Easy on the eyes, if you know what I mean. To this day, I think he is the handsomest man I've ever laid my eyes on. His hair isn't dark anymore, and he doesn't stand as tall as he once did, but he is still the man I love."

Her grandma's eyes had filled with tears as she remembered their younger days, probably wishing they were young again. Now the journey was almost over for them. Grandpa had been sick with cancer, and Grandma was beginning to show signs of dementia, yet the memories of her husband had not faded.

"My child, if you ever find someone that makes you feel the way Eley made me feel, you better grab him, because it only comes around once in a lifetime. Remember that," her grandma had said as she patted Melanie on the arm. "Oh, I don't have to tell you. You'll know when the right man comes along."

Melanie thought it would be wonderful to know in your heart that a person was the one you were meant to be with. Grandma must have been right, because they were married seventy-two years and raised nine children together. Melanie missed her grandparents. It was strange the way they died only six months apart. Her grandma died first. Melanie heard the doctor tell her mother that Grandpa just gave up after that. He was buried exactly six months later. The doctor said he literally died of a broken heart. He was diagnosed with "failure to thrive." At the time, she had never heard of it, but since she had become a nurse, she had heard of it often. Melanie smiled at the thought of them together in heaven, him tall and handsome, and she with sweaty palms, flushing face, and racing heart. Melanie giggled. Yeah, God, send me a man that can do that to me, and I'll know it's for real. I promise not to ask for a sign ever again.

Joan and Melanie had an ongoing joke about Melanie always asking for "a sign." Joan asked her one day, "How many signs do you need?" She counted off about three signs that were obvious it was not a good relationship with James. Melanie recalled riding down the road from the beach one day last summer, and on a big billboard in huge, black letters on a white background, it read, "Well, you asked for a sign," and right underneath that line, in huge letters, was "God." Melanie broke out laughing when she saw it. So far, she was still waiting for "a sign." Now more than ever, she needed a sign. She was really confused about the situation with Ron and Morgan. She had hoped it wouldn't be a problem, but to deny it wasn't a concern would be foolish.

Melanie hadn't felt sweaty palms when Ron was around, and she didn't think he made her face flush, but she did feel deep feelings for him. She doubted things like flushing and sweaty palms really ever happened, even though she believed it happened to Grandma. Melanie chuckled, thinking back on that day. Grandma was full of wisdom, she thought. She wished she were still around. Melanie thought of Morgan and wondered what her grandma would think if she knew Morgan were pregnant by a black man. She'd been raised in a time when blacks and whites didn't mix socially. Things had really changed since then, Melanie thought; at least for most people. Some people were still hanging onto the old ways and would never change their thinking. Just this weekend, Melanie and Morgan had gone shopping in town and noticed people smirking and pointing at them. Morgan heard one lady say, "There goes that girl that's having a black baby."

White people stared and smirked at Morgan, and black people stared and smirked at her. Everywhere Morgan went, they made comments about her pregnancy. Melanie took it harder than Morgan did. Morgan ignored them, but Melanie wanted to confront them. It was not that she was pregnant and unmarried that bothered them; it was the fact the daddy was black. It was the same with black people in this town; they resented a white girl being pregnant by a black man. Melanie had seen some young black girls harassing Morgan about being pregnant by a black guy. One black girl working in a clothing store had been rude to Morgan, making a comment about leaving the black men alone for real women. A good friend of Melanie's at work, Valerie, a black nurse she had worked with for years, admitted she would be furious if she found out her daughter was dating a white guy. She went on and on about how she didn't believe in interracial relationships. Her honesty had surprised Melanie. Another co-worker referred to a black man as a "colored man" in Valerie's company, and it offended her to the point that she blatantly asked the co-worker, "What color was the man? Red?

Yellow? Blue?" It had embarrassed the co-worker, and for a moment, she didn't know how to respond then Valerie laughed as if she were joking and said, "Oh, you mean a black man. I wasn't sure what color you were talking about."

Both races in the community thought Morgan and Daryl were wrong. They couldn't go anywhere in public together because people were rude to them. His family didn't want her at their house, and Daryl didn't feel comfortable at Morgan's. It was hard on them, and for that Melanie was sorry. She could only imagine how it would be to be in love with someone and feel like the whole world is against you. Melanie didn't think she was prejudiced, but she had never been one to make waves, and this certainly was making waves.

She didn't think God looked down on them for loving each other because they were different races. Sometimes, when she encountered people's ignorance, she wanted to shout, "Show me in the Bible where it says anything about interracial relationships! Show me in the Bible where it says two people of different races cannot bear children together!"

Why could men go into service and overseas and bring back a Vietnamese wife or a German wife or a Korean wife, and all was well and dandy, but a white female couldn't have a black boyfriend without being ridiculed off the face of the earth. Why was there a difference? How many times had she heard a man say how beautiful Mexican women are, but white men became absolutely irate when they saw a white woman with a black man. Men had a double standard about almost everything. Melanie could see them fuming when they looked at Morgan. It was obvious they despised the thought of a white girl with a black man. They would stare, a cold, solemn look on their faces. Melanie noticed the way people looked at Morgan now that the truth was out. Some people didn't speak at all—just gawked at her.

Another time, Melanie, Morgan, and Kevin were in a local restaurant when she saw a lady staring at them. Melanie recognized the lady as someone that worked in the local supermarket where they bought groceries. The lady stared at them for several minutes. Melanie took it as long as she could. She was not sure if she was staring at Morgan or Kevin, but regardless, she could not get enough. Maybe she was staring at Kevin, since he no longer was able to eat neatly. Melanie constantly had to tell him to wipe his mouth or hands. He mixed his food up until it looked like a three-year-old was eating it. Melanie was not sure who she was staring at, but she caught the lady's gaze and bulged her eyes and stared at the lady as hard as she could. The lady turned her head quickly.

Morgan was sitting across from Melanie, and she busted out laughing. "Mama what are you doing?" she asked, laughing.

"I'm staring at that woman who can't stop staring at us," Melanie said loudly enough for the woman to hear her. The woman looked into her plate for the rest of her meal, afraid to look their way anymore. Morgan shook her head, still laughing. Kevin laughed, too, but Melanie was sure he didn't understand why they were laughing. His ability to know the difference between a joke and truth had also been lost since the accident. That was a real shame because he had always been a real teaser. Melanie missed his personality and practical jokes. She missed a lot of things about the old Kevin.

A few of Melanie's friends had voiced unfavorable opinions. Some were more discreet than others. Another co-worker, a white nurse, fell back in her chair and shouted, "Oh, my God!" when Melanie told her about Morgan's pregnancy. The co-worker had gone on and on about what a disgrace it was and that she couldn't have stood it if her daughter were pregnant by a black man. A few months later, her daughter was pregnant and unmarried, but the father was white. You would think the girl had won an Academy Award the way her mother carried on. She was so proud. She told everybody about her daughter's pregnancy, yet every time she was around Melanie, she shook her head at the mention of Morgan's pregnancy.

Another co-worker had invited Melanie and Morgan to attend her church. Melanie told her they were attending a nondenominational church where all races are welcome. Melanie told her about Morgan and the coming biracial baby and said that was one reason they had chosen their particular church. For a moment, the lady was quiet then slowly, she wrinkled her nose and said hesitantly, "Oh, we don't have any of those at our church."

It was the way she had said "those" that bothered Melanie most. It was almost as if she didn't consider blacks people. Melanie had liked the lady up to that point. Again, she had called herself a Christian. Melanie was finding out some Christians had double standards. She never felt the same towards the lady after that. Melanie also had people tell her it would never, ever happen with their daughter. They did not know what their child would do, in spite of all the talking and rules. She, too, never thought Morgan would end up pregnant by a black guy.

Friends and co-workers would go on and on. "My daughter knows I would kill her if she pregnant by a black guy," they'd say, and then they'd laugh like it was a big joke. Why did people say that? They weren't going to kill their own child. Melanie wanted to scream at them, "Shut up! Your child is just like all other kids, and you don't know what he or she may or may not do by the time he or she is grown. You may have to make the same choices I had to make, and I hope you choose your child, just like I did."

Blah, blah, blah, blah! Melanie was tired of hearing how perfect everybody thought their kids were when she knew for a fact some of the girls were seeing black guys, just as Morgan was. She also knew there were white boys seeing black girls, but you never heard talk of that. A few times, Melanie wanted to blurt it out, but she didn't. What they thought and what their kids did was none of her business. Still, they made it their business to share their opinion about Morgan.

Melanie saw a lot of her friends in a different light now, and unfortunately, the light was dim. She had learned the difference between true friends and acquaintances. True friends didn't judge and they loved people in spite of differing beliefs. Sometimes Melanie tried to put herself in the other person's place and them in hers. She didn't think she would feel any different about them, even though in the past she was sure she had stared at interracial couples and wondered why they put themselves through the torment and harassment. She thought it would have been just as easy to fall in love with someone their own race. Certainly, it'd make life a whole lot simpler for them. She had gotten angry with Morgan and said, "There are millions of white boys out there that would love you. Why on earth did you have to pick a black boy?" She went on and on about this cute guy and that cute guy that would have been perfect for her, but, oh no, she had to pick a black boy to fall in love with. Melanie could not understand it, and it did upset her.

Yes, she would have preferred Morgan choose someone white. It would have made both of their lives a lot easier. Melanie had seen good looking black men; some she may have even dated if things were different, but things were the way they were, and she was not about to go against local society. She would stick with life as she had always known it, and she resented Morgan for pulling her into an area she didn't want to be a part of. Yes, she did wish the daddy was white. Was that so wrong? Melanie didn't think so.

Melanie prayed for the strength to get through this ordeal. She was afraid, and she admitted it. Sometimes she and Morgan lashed out at each other and both ended up with their feelings hurt. Morgan told Melanie she didn't fall in love with the color of Daryl's skin, she fell in love with the person. Again, Melanie felt Morgan should not have opened herself up to fall in love with him knowing it would upset a lot of people, especially her family. In all fairness, Morgan was raised in a time when race was not an issue. She played sports and was around black boys all the time. She had best friends that were black, and Melanie had no problem with that; so did she, but she knew not to fall in love with a black man.

How could Morgan do that to them? Dan would never get over it, his family would never get over it, and some of their friends would never get over it. Melanie accepted it because she had to, but she was not sure she'd ever get over it, either. She did not want to spend the rest of her life looking over her shoulder to see who was staring and gossiping about the white girl with a biracial child. It burned Melanie up thinking about what people did when they saw them in public. She resented their attitudes and stares. She wondered how many more times she would have to glare at someone. Melanie smiled again, proud of herself for embarrassing the woman that day. It wouldn't be the last time she defended Morgan and her grandchild. She was getting stronger with each passing day. By the time the baby got here, she'd be able to handle about anything, she assured herself. Then she thought of Ron, and was not so sure.

Chapter Eighteen

*I*t was almost time for Morgan to have her baby, and she was getting very uncomfortable. She told Melanie she was going to walk around the block hoping it would cause her to go into labor.

Melanie smiled. "The baby will come when the baby is ready."

"Well, I'm ready for this baby to be ready," Morgan replied.

Melanie laughed. "Good luck. If you go into labor, you're only a few blocks from the hospital; just walk on over and admit yourself."

"Believe me, I will be happy to do that," Morgan answered as she went out the door.

Melanie shook her head. She didn't even know this was the easy part; wait until she actually did go into labor. She didn't know what uncomfortable was until she started labor pains. Melanie shivered just remembering the ordeal. "Glad it's not me," she sighed.

A couple of nights later, Melanie was upstairs when Morgan hollered for her. "Mama!"

Melanie dropped the clothes she was folding and went to her door. She was not sure she had really heard something.

"Mama!"

Melanie went to Morgan's room. Morgan was sitting on the edge of the bed. "Mama, I think I am having labor pains." Morgan made a sound halfway between a laugh and a cry.

"Let's get you to the hospital now." Melanie smiled nervously.

Melanie was scared and anxious. She helped Morgan get the suitcase out of the closet. Morgan held her stomach as if another pain had started. Pain mixed with fright and happiness on her face. She made the strange sound again.

"Come on, sweetie; let's get you to the hospital and bring this baby into the world. I do believe he's ready."

Morgan nodded. "I think he is." She took out her cell phone and dialed a number. "I'm going to the hospital; I'm in labor," she said anxiously. "Come as soon as you can. I love you. Bye."

Melanie knew it was the baby's daddy. Melanie felt strange that she still had not met the daddy after all these months. She would certainly get to meet him tonight, she thought.

Morgan doubled over with another pain. "Mama!"

"It's going to be all right, hon," Melanie assured her.

Melanie called ahead to let the hospital know they were on the way. When they arrived at the emergency entrance, there were two nurses waiting with a wheelchair. They got her into the emergency room while Melanie parked the car. The labor and delivery room was set up much like a bedroom at home. Things had really changed since Melanie gave birth to her children. Back then there was a labor room and a separate delivery room; neither looked like a bedroom. They looked like hospital rooms with charts of dilation and that alone was enough to scare anyone, Melanie thought.

Morgan settled into her bed and waited for another pain. She looked at the clock. Daryl still wasn't there. She looked worried.

"He'll be here shortly," Melanie assured her. "It is a twenty-minute drive, not counting traffic," she said.

Morgan looked scared.

Melanie took her hand. "Just think, it will all be over soon, and you'll have that little person you've been waiting for in your arms, not in your stomach keeping you up all night kicking your insides." She kissed Morgan on the head.

Secretly, she was scared to death herself. As a nurse, she knew all the things that could go wrong, but she prayed it would be a normal delivery. Morgan had another pain and squeezed Melanie's hand tightly. After a minute it was gone, and she relaxed again, loosening her grip. The door opened slowly, and a tall, young, black man peeped inside. Melanie looked at him and then at Morgan. Morgan's face lit up. She had tears in her eyes, and she wiped them with her free hand.

The young man walked slowly to the other side of the bed. He took hold of Morgan's other hand. Melanie reached out to shake his hand. "I'm Morgan's mama," Melanie said, smiling. "It's nice to meet you."

He smiled back and shook her hand. "I'm Daryl," he said shyly.

"I figured," she replied, still smiling at him.

Melanie thought it odd that she had never met him before now. Looking back, she wondered why she had not tried before. She had made a lot of mistakes, and that was just another one. She should have suggested to Morgan that she wanted to meet him earlier, but she had not. It was almost like meeting him meant she accepted him as the father, and up until now, she was not sure she was ready for that.

She looked into his eyes when she spoke to him. He was dark. His skin was almost black. He had pretty eyes, she thought, and a nice smile. Then again, she did love brown eyes. He was tall and slim. He was a nice looking young man. He seemed quiet and shy, almost afraid to talk. Melanie was sure it was just as awkward for him as it was for her meeting for the first time in a labor room. Melanie thought maybe she should leave them alone for a few minutes, so she made an excuse to go out. "I'm going in the hall to make a phone call," she said. "I'll be right back in a few minutes."

He nodded. "Okay," he said.

She squeezed Morgan's hand. "I'll be right back."

Morgan nodded.

She went into the hall and closed the door. Now is when I wished I smoked, she thought. Melanie walked down the hall and sat in the waiting room for fifteen minutes. When Melanie returned, Morgan was having a hard labor pain. Morgan reached out to Melanie and took hold of her hand. Morgan buried her face on top of her mama's hand. Her other hand held Daryl's hand. He looked as if he didn't know what to do. He was scared to death for Morgan. She was sure he was uncomfortable, too, because he knew Morgan's family disapproved of their relationship. He laid his head on her arm as she squeezed their hands firmly. Morgan had tears running down her face but was not making any noise. She was being really strong and doing very well, not crying out or making a fuss.

The nurse came in to check the baby's position. She told Morgan to hold her legs open; the baby was in position. Morgan was tired and in a lot of pain. She told Daryl to hold her leg.

He made some comment and laid his head down on the rail, looking the other way. "I can't," he muttered, still looking away.

"Hold my leg!" Morgan threatened, her voice like something from *The Exorcist.*

Melanie expected to see Morgan's head spin around. She smiled to herself. You go, girl. You need to make him feel the pain, too.

Melanie grabbed Morgan's other leg to help support it. Dr. Dayton was there, ready to deliver the baby, as he began to emerge into his new world.

"Wait for the pain to start and then push as hard as you can," Dr. Dayton said.

Morgan waited anxiously, and then the labor pain hit again. Morgan squeezed Melanie's hand so tight it felt like it was in a vise. Melanie glanced over at Daryl; he had his head down on the rail with his face turned away. He didn't look like he was feeling too good at the moment.

Good! Melanie thought. You got the good end of the deal. She turned her attention back to Morgan.

Morgan was pushing as hard as she could, making loud groans until she was out of breath and the pain ceased again. Melanie saw the baby's head emerging and grew even more nervous with each tense moment. She was almost as anxious as Morgan was to get this over with.

Morgan took a deep breath as the next pain hit and squeezed their hands again as she pushed with all the strength in her body. Her face was red and sweating. She had tears in her eyes and a scared look on her face. "It hurts," she cried angrily, like a helpless child.

Melanie felt sorry for her, but this was out of her control; there was nothing she could do to ease the pain this time. Melanie rubbed Morgan's hair. "It's almost over, honey. Just a couple more pushes, and he'll be here."

Another pain and Morgan pushed hard again.

"You're doing great. Here comes the head; keep pushing," Dr. Dalton said.

Morgan pushed until the baby's head was completely out then she stopped for another breath. The baby waited patiently for Morgan to finish the job. Melanie looked at the baby's head, anxiously inspecting every detail—head, face, mouth, ears, nose—they all looked normal. It was some relief; still, she was so anxious she could hardly breathe. Things could still go wrong, and she could not relax until the baby was safely out and Morgan was okay. Melanie glanced at Daryl. If she hadn't been so worried, she would have found him very comical. His face was further down into the rail, and she could swear he was pale. The corner of her lip couldn't help but turn up for a second. Melanie felt for Morgan, laying there, the baby half-in and half-out. She remembered the pain all too well, but there was something worse about watching Morgan go through it.

Suddenly, Morgan blurted angrily, "What is he doing?"

The next pain hit, and Morgan and the doctor got ready.

"Push. That's right; he's coming. Good girl! Keep on; don't stop, he's almost here."

With that, the baby's shoulders popped through and the doctor helped him the rest of the way out. Melanie eyes scanned every inch of him.

His head—normal, black hair—not surprising. Eyes, ears, nose—perfect. Arms, hands, fingers—all there. Abdomen, penis—yep, it's a boy, just like they said. Legs—good. Feet—wow! Look at those feet! Took after his mama. Melanie hoped he would be light-skinned since his mama was a green-eyed blonde. His skin was light, but it would probably darken some in the next few weeks. He was beautiful.

Melanie smiled and breathed again, letting all the anxiety leave her body. She couldn't find anything wrong with him; he looked perfect. Melanie started to breathe normally again for the first time since Morgan had had her first labor pain.

The OBGYN team started working on him, suctioning and cleaning him. After a few seconds, he started to cry; everyone laughed then and relaxed a little.

Melanie kissed Morgan on the head. "You did it, kiddo."

Morgan sat up to look at him and started smiling.

"You laugh now, but a few minutes ago, you wanted to know what he was doing," Melanie teased.

Morgan laughed.

Daryl had finally raised his head and smiled as he watched the nurses clean the baby up. He was still holding Morgan's hand. Melanie smiled, Morgan had held her hand just a little closer and tighter than she did his. Sometimes, no one can replace your mama, and childbirth just happened to be one of them. Melanie felt surprisingly happy and relieved it was over.

The nurse picked the baby up to carry him to another table to clean him and check him out. Melanie instinctively followed, holding her hands underneath the nurse's hands as if she were afraid the nurse was going to drop him. In a few moments, the nurse brought him back and laid him in Morgan's arms.

"I present you with little Noah," she said, smiling.

Melanie watched Morgan hold her baby. She was happier than Melanie had ever seen her. She was happy for Morgan— and for Daryl. He was smiling from ear to ear as he held Noah's finger.

Melanie felt something inside like she had never known, not even when her own children were born. Her heart felt so full and she had so much love for the little person she had only known for a few minutes. Tears stung her eyes when she looked at him. They already had a bond that nothing would ever come between.

Again, Melanie felt she should give Morgan and Daryl some time alone with the baby so she excused herself. She would make some phone calls and let family know Noah had arrived safe and sound. Melanie phoned Morgan's dad and informed him of Noah's arrival. Of course, he had a few negative comments, as Melanie had expected. That was just his nature. Still, he was concerned for Morgan and the baby's well being, and glad everything went okay. Dan loved Morgan, and he would eventually love Noah. He just didn't know it yet. He had a soft side. She had seen it just recently, when he broke down and cried with her at the doctor's office when Kevin couldn't make his sentences come out the way he wanted and got frustrated. They had both cried; their hearts were breaking for him, and they knew he needed help, but they didn't know how to help him. She also knew Dan loved her and the children; he just sometimes didn't know how to show it. She couldn't deny he had been good in a lot of ways and once he met Noah, his heart would change. He had always loved babies, and he would love Noah just as he loved Kevin and Morgan.

Next, Melanie called her mama and daddy. Her mama was glad to hear Morgan and Noah were doing well. She said to tell Morgan she loved her and would see her soon. Melanie called Joan to let her know she was a great-aunt and then Charles to let him know he was a great-uncle. Both were glad Morgan and the baby were doing fine and sent their love.

Finally, Melanie called Ron. She wasn't sure how he would react. She knew he had been distant to Morgan during her pregnancy and felt it was because the daddy was black. She knew in her heart he was prejudiced, but she didn't want to admit it. When Melanie tried to talk to him about it, he denied any hard feelings towards her daughter. Still, Melanie and Morgan both felt the coolness. Melanie hated to think she was thinking about marrying a man that could not accept her family and love them unconditionally. Maybe with time he would accept them for who they were not what they were.

When the phone rang, she took a deep breath. "Hi!" she said, cheerful and excited.

"Hi, sweetie," he answered pleasantly. "What's up?"

"I am calling to tell you I am officially a grandma!"

"Oh! You are? And how is everybody?"

"Everybody is fine. Morgan is doing well, and so is the baby. She named him Noah. I think that is a pretty name," Melanie said happily.

"Well, good. I'm glad they are doing okay." His voice seemed a little strained.

Melanie wondered if she were just imagining his strained reaction. Maybe she was looking too hard to find something. I am going back to the room in a few minutes, but I wanted to give them some time alone with the new baby."

"Them?"

"Yes, the baby's daddy is here, too."

"Oh? And how is he doing?"

"Great."

"That's good."

"Well, I'll talk to you later tonight. I'll call when I leave the hospital."

"Okay, sweetie. I look forward to hearing from you." His voice sounded better now that they were off the subject of Morgan and the baby.

It was not her imagination. He did sound different after she changed the subject. He definitely had some issues.

Some of Morgan's friends visited her at the hospital and took all kinds of pictures. Some took pictures with a camera, some with camera phones, and some with videos. She had never seen so many flashes and people saying smile. Most of Morgan's friends had stuck by her, giving her the support she needed. Melanie was thankful for youth and youth's ability to accept change. Sometimes she thought young people lived by the serenity prayer much better than older people—especially the part about accepting the things they couldn't change and the wisdom to know the difference. Some people never accepted things they couldn't change. Dan, for instance. He couldn't make Noah white; would he accept him the way he was? Melanie didn't know the answer.

After two days in the hospital, Morgan went home. Little Noah had everything a baby could possibly need. He had the bassinet his uncle, mama, and Joan's kids had slept in when they were first born. Other than that, he had everything new. Most was blue, of course. It was a good thing he didn't turn out to be a she.

Ron had not visited Morgan in the hospital, which surprised Melanie a little. He was usually so dedicated about visiting people in the hospital, but she knew he had been busy at work, so she could justify that.

Chapter Nineteen

O ver the next couple of months, everything went pretty
   smoothly. Melanie's family had welcomed little Noah with
open arms. Dan's family had not been quite as accepting, but that
was because Dan had not come to terms with Noah yet. Once Dan
accepted Noah, so would the rest of his family. He had not given
them a chance to know Noah. Melanie's heart broke when Morgan told her she was not invited to the Hutchins' family reunion
because her dad didn't want her to bring Noah. Melanie felt Dan
wanted to be a part of Noah's life, but worried about what others
thought. Dan would have to make the same decision she'd
made—did he want a daughter and grandchild, or not? It was as
simple as that. He had been around every week to visit for a few
minutes and had held Noah each time. Melanie knew Noah was
working on his heart; he was just a hard nut to crack—but he
would. She was sure of it; she just didn't know how long it was
going to take. Each day he missed with Noah was his loss.

    It wasn't easy because everywhere they went, people stared
and made comments. Melanie saw people whispering when
they were in public, just as they had when Morgan was pregnant. As before, the men were the worst. When they saw Noah
was biracial, their whole expression changed. It was not easy
for Melanie to see the prejudices they encountered from both
races. She knew it bothered Morgan, too, even though she
rarely said anything about it. She had accepted it or was deny-
ing it; Melanie was not sure which.

    Sometimes Morgan would come home and tell Melanie
about the comments people made. It was unbelievable how
cruel grown people could be. Melanie had expected it, but actually seeing it was hard. It cut deep knowing people resented an
innocent child. The crazier people acted, the more Melanie tried
to protect them, but she couldn't. Noah would grow up in a
prejudiced world, just as she had done, and her parents before
her, and her grandparents before them.

Melanie knew everybody was not prejudiced, but most of the people in this town were and always would be. They didn't want to change. White men seemed to think black men were paying them back for the slave days by taking their white women. Melanie didn't believe that; she just thought people wanted to live without having to divide between black and white. She didn't think Daryl was thinking about getting back at Morgan's ancestors by getting her pregnant; he fell in love with her—what man wouldn't? Morgan didn't look at people as white or black; she never had. Noah would be the one to suffer the most, Melanie feared.

Chapter Twenty

$\mathcal{M}$elanie's birthday was fast approaching. She would soon be forty-four years old. Noah was a few months old. Morgan had turned twenty a couple of months ago and had decided to go back to school to become a nurse. Melanie was happy about that, but wondered if she would stick with it this time. Melanie prayed she would because she needed to be able to take care of herself and Noah. Morgan seemed determined to get her degree this time. She was smart and could do it if she wanted it badly enough. It would be twice as hard now that she had a baby, but not impossible.

Ron had a special night planned for Melanie's birthday. He wanted her to dress extra nicely because he was taking her to a super-nice restaurant. Melanie put on a white sundress that showed off her tanned skin. She thought about the "little black dress," but decided against it. Just enough cleavage showed to make it a little seductive.

"Perfect," she said, looking at herself in the mirror. "This ought to get his attention." She splashed on a little perfume and put on some lipstick. "Okay. I'm ready. I've done the best I can to impress you, Mr. Ron," she said out loud to the mirror.

Melanie wondered if he would buy her something for her birthday or just take her out for a meal. Her ex never gave her presents, and she was always a little hurt by that. Occasionally, he left her a little money on the kitchen bar, but never a gift to unwrap. He would say, "It's the thought that counts," and she would think, "Yeah, the thought that you didn't take the time to buy me a gift." She once read somewhere, "If you don't expect anything then you can't be disappointed." She'd lived by that rule, and it worked. It wasn't near as hurtful if she didn't expect anything.

Ron arrived around 6:30. He was dressed in a pair of black pants and a blue shirt. He looked very handsome, and his blue eyes were enhanced by his shirt. His face lit up when he saw Melanie. She smiled. She had succeeded at her mission.

"Hi," he said, smiling.

"Hi, good-looking," she said.

"My, my, don't you look spiffy!" he said.

"Spiffy? That's the best you can do?" she teased.

"You know, spiffy to me is beautiful."

"Oh, yeah, I remember you telling me that once. Okay, thank you," she smiled. "You look spiffy, too."

"Are you telling me I am beautiful? Actually, I prefer to go with 'good looking,' if you don't mind."

"To me you are beautiful—a beautiful person," she said.

"Then beautiful it is, and I take that as a high compliment."

She had never seen him look so handsome or happy. Ron put his arms around her and squeezed her tight. Melanie felt warm and happy, and she held him close for a long moment. After a few moments enjoying the closeness, he let go and looked at her as if he truly loved her. It felt good.

"Now, are you ready for a special birthday?"

"I am," she answered anxiously, like a kid.

"Well, let's not waste anymore time because we have reservations."

"We do? Where?" she asked.

"That's a surprise; you'll see when you get there," he answered.

The restaurant was a fancy place on the waterfront. The lights reflected on the water where boats were docked for the night. The restaurant had a glass enclosed dining room that gave one the feeling of dining outside. They had a table next to the waterfront windows. It was beautiful. She was very impressed. Ron ordered wine. After making small talk for about forty-five minutes, Ron took out a small box and sat it on the table.

Melanie stared at it, wondering if he had bought her a pair of earrings.

"Open it," he said, his smile flashing in the candlelight.

Melanie slowly took the box in her hands. "Thank you," she said softly.

"Thank me for what? You haven't opened it yet," he said, grinning mischievously.

"Thank you for all of this," she motioned.

"You are welcome. Now, open your present," he said anxiously.

She smiled and started to unwrap the box. Her mind was going in a million directions. It was a very small box. What if? No, he wouldn't. But what if he had? Melanie was sure he hadn't. Melanie slowly unwrapped the box. It was a beautiful, dark red velvet box with an emblem of a sparking diamond on top that glittered in the light. Just as I thought—diamond earrings. "I don't know what's inside, but if it's anything like the box, it is beautiful," she said aloud. "Thank you," Melanie said again, looking down at the beautiful red box.

"Thank me for what? You still haven't opened the present," Ron said, laughing. "My goodness! Next time, I won't buy you a present; I'll just give you a box."

Melanie looked at Ron and then back down at the box. Slowly she lifted the top of the red box. What she saw next almost took her breath away. Inside, on a black velvet stand, was a beautiful diamond engagement ring. It was about a carat and sparkled with every turn as she twisted it in each direction. Melanie was surprised, although she had thought about it. Part of her had hoped he would propose and part of her had hoped he wouldn't. Now, though, lost in the mood, she definitely wanted Ron to propose. Melanie laughed as she held the ring, still in the box, up to the candle to watch it sparkle in the light. She stared at the ring, lost for words. She had mixed emotions. She was happy, confused, ecstatic, hesitant, rejoicing, but most of all, surprised. They had talked a little about marriage, but he never officially proposed. Obviously, that was next.

Ron took Melanie's hand and looked her in the eyes. "The day I met you, my life changed for the better. More than anything, I want to spend the rest of my life with you. I want us to grow old together and sit in rocking chairs on the front porch when we're gray." Ron paused as he looked in Melanie's eyes, searching to find the same feelings. Melanie's eyes filled to the edges and spilled gently onto her cheeks. She smiled tenderly at him.

"Melanie, will you marry me?" Ron squeezed her hands a little tighter as he waited for her answer.

Melanie stared back into Ron's blue eyes. She knew she cared deeply for him and was sure he was what she had been waiting for. Ron was holding her hands, waiting for what seemed like an eternity.

Melanie smiled. "Yes, I will marry you," she said softly.

An older couple at a table nearby had witnessed the whole proposal. They tried not to be obvious, but clapped softly when Melanie said yes, then quickly turned back to give Ron his privacy. Ron took the ring out of the box and placed it on her left finger. Melanie loved the ring. The ring slid on her finger with ease. She felt a new closeness to him.

"I will make you happy, and I will never hurt you," Ron promised as he kissed her gently on the lips.

For a instant, Melanie thought of Morgan and Noah then quickly returned to the present. "I love you, too," she answered. She had finally found someone that truly loved her.

Melanie thought of her grandma. She wished she could have met Ron; she would have liked him. Then she thought of Grandma's theory on meeting one's soul mate. What about the flushed face, sweaty palms, and racing heart she had expected to experience—like her grandma had spoken of? Even though none of those things had happened, Melanie knew Ron was her soul mate, and Melanie didn't believe in love at first sight, anyway. How many times did that ever happen?

Once—to Grandma, she thought with a smile. Melanie shook off the thought of Grandma Rose's love predictions and leaned over and kissed Ron. "You are full of surprises, aren't you?" she said, holding her hand out proudly to admire her ring.

"Only when I need to be," he answered, smiling.

"You sure took me by surprise."

"A pleasant surprise, I hope."

"Oh, yes. A very pleasant surprise," she replied, still beaming.

They kissed again, and then Ron held his glass up for a toast. Melanie followed, holding her glass up to his.

"This is to the spiffiest woman," Ron winked at her, "I have ever met, and I promise to make you very happy in the future." Ron tapped Melanie's glass with his, and they each took a sip.

"My turn," Melanie said. She held her glass up again. "To the sweetest man I have ever met. Thank you for coming into my life." She tapped his glass with hers, and they took another sip.

Melanie was happy with her engagement. It was the right thing for them. Her only hesitation was his issues with Morgan and Noah. Melanie felt confident time would take care of all that, and Ron would learn to love Morgan and Noah and forget about race and prejudice. The rest of the night was wonderful. They drank wine, danced, and talked for hours.

When the night finally ended, Melanie felt on top of the world, but Morgan and Noah kept interrupting her thoughts. She wondered how Morgan would accept the news. She knew Morgan wanted her to be happy, and for the most part, Ron and Morgan got along fine. Morgan just thought Ron was a little distant sometimes, and Melanie knew he was. Time would take care of that, she assured herself once again.

When Melanie got home, she went upstairs to show Morgan her engagement ring and tell her about Ron's proposal. Melanie peeped in her room to see if she was asleep and Morgan discreetly turned her face and wiped away her tears. Morgan was a private person at times and didn't want people to see her vulnerable side. She had gotten that from Dan. Melanie felt it was just the blues, like everybody has at times. Morgan would tell her what was wrong when and if she was ready.

As Melanie walked over to the bed, Morgan smiled. "What did you get for your birthday?"

Melanie smiled and brought her hand up to display the engagement ring. Part of her felt guilty because she knew Morgan wanted to be married, too. Morgan grabbed Melanie's hand and brought the diamond up for a closer view. Her eyes widened, and Melanie knew the diamond met her daughter's approval.

"Oh, my God, Mama! It's beautiful! Let me try it on."

Melanie slid the ring off for Morgan to try on. Morgan took the ring then remembered her left hand was swollen and put it on her right finger. "It's gorgeous."

"Thank you," Melanie said, slowly picking up Morgan's left hand.

"Oh, my God. Your fingers are blue. Are they broken? What happened to you?"

"I fell down the stairs and caught my hand on the rails. My fingers got hung up in the rails somehow," Morgan said, looking down at her hand as she talked.

"Oh, my goodness. Did you hurt yourself anywhere else?"

"My elbow is bruised a little, I think."

"Let me see."

Morgan slowly pulled up her sleeve.

Melanie gasped. "How did you bruise the inside of your arm so badly?"

"I don't know. I just did."

"Maybe I need to take you to have your arm x-rayed."

"No, Mama; it's not broken, just bruised."

Morgan handed Melanie her ring back, and she slid it on her left finger. "I'm glad you had a nice birthday."

"Thanks, sweetie."

"I'm worried about your fingers."

"They'll be okay; now I want to go to bed, okay?"

"It was a blessing you didn't have Noah in your arms when you fell."

"Yes, it is. 'Night, Mama. I love you."

"'Night. I love you, too."

Melanie went up to her room and went to bed exhausted. It had been a full day. She couldn't get Morgan off her mind. There was something wrong. Morgan rarely cried, and if she did, something was really wrong.

Chapter Twenty-one

*R*on wanted to get married soon, so they began to make plans for a wedding. It would be a small wedding, with just family and a few friends. Melanie asked Joan and her mama to help plan the wedding. They were happy she had finally found someone special.

"You must have gotten 'the sign,'" Joan teased as they talked about wedding plans.

"Yeah, 'the sign' is I just turned forty-four, and I'm not married," Melanie laughed.

"Age has nothing to do with happiness," her mama added, smiling, but making a point just the same.

"I know, Mama. I'm only kidding," Melanie said, laughing.

As usual, being the kid sister, Joan kept edging Melanie on as she had always done, especially when Melanie just wanted her to be quiet.

" 'The sign'? I want to know if you got 'the sign'." Joan teased, a little louder and firmer, putting her hand on her hip and waiting for an answer.

Melanie looked at Joan and said, "I believe the correct term is 'a' sign, not 'the' sign."

"What the heck? 'a' sign. There, are you happy? Did you see 'a' sign?"

Melanie ignored her and started talking with her mother about wedding dresses.

Joan persisted. "Well? Did you?"

Melanie stopped talking to her mother and put her hand to her face and thought a moment. "Oh, no!" Melanie blurted loudly.

"What?" Joan asked, startled.

Their mama waited and looked from one to the other. She never knew what to expect with the two of them together. Good thing Charles wasn't here because it would be triple trouble. Her mama use to call them that sometimes when they were up to something. "Here comes triple trouble," she'd say when the three of them were ganging up together to ask for something.

Daddy would agree with her. "Yeah, they are either up to something, or they've already done something," he'd say, pulling his cigarette out of his mouth, his eyes narrowing, waiting for them to pop the deal, or the confession, whichever it may be.

"What? What?" Joan asked.

Melanie bent over, laughing. Joan and her mama started laughing, too, at Melanie's hysterics. It was contagious.

Melanie fell to her knees beside the couch, looked up to heaven, and put her hands in the air. She was laughing so hard her hands kept falling to the floor, but she would put them up again each time.

Finally she gathered her composure enough to continue. "Grandma, please forgive me. I'm marrying a man and I didn't see 'the' sign, 'a' sign, or 'any' sign," she said between spurts of laughter.

Joan dropped to the floor beside Melanie, pushing her to the floor. "I knew it!" she said, laughing. "After all those years of asking for 'a sign', you agreed to marry a man without one. Are you crazy?"

"Well, I don't know. Maybe I better ask Grandma about that. She didn't tell me what to do if I never got 'a sign'," Melanie joked. "Maybe I'm suppose to stay single the rest of my life."

"I always heard don't tease the dead," her mama joked. "You don't want to jinx your wedding, do you?"

"Heaven's, no!" Joan answered. "It's probably the last chance she'll get."

"I hope it is," Melanie said as she stood, pulled Joan up, and then let her go so she'd fall back down. Melanie laughed and put her hand out again, this time pulling Joan up.

"Straighten up, girls; we have a wedding to plan," Her mama reminded them.

"She started it," Melanie said.

"Did not," Joan retaliated.

"Did, too; now behave, or I'll be forty five and still not married," Melanie said. "We have a lot to do in the next few weeks."

"You didn't get 'a sign'," Joan sang under her breath.

"I don't care. I'm getting married anyway," Melanie sang back.

"Not everybody is lucky enough to get 'a sign' like your grandma did," her mama said in Melanie's defense. "You have to know it in your heart, like I did with your daddy. Remember, we've been married almost sixty years," she said proudly.

"That's right," Melanie said as she picked up the wedding list. "Now let's get busy and plan a wedding. I'm getting married." Melanie turned to Joan with a little smirk. "With or without 'a sign'."

Joan and her mama laughed.

Melanie sat down and picked up the ink pen to make notes, still laughing a little at all the joking, when a slightly serious thought crept through her mind. "Why didn't He send me 'a sign'? I've always asked Him for one."

Chapter Twenty-two

*A*s the next few weeks went by, Melanie felt Ron was not quite what he should be in Morgan's presence. She felt he ignored Morgan and often acted as if she weren't even there. He barely looked at Morgan when he talked to her, and he didn't have anything much to do with Noah.

When Melanie picked up Noah and held him, Ron acted as if he didn't want Noah to touch him. He even leaned to the side to keep from touching him on the couch when she had him in her arms. Melanie noticed everything. Ron always played with other kids. He never did with Noah. If Ron continued to have hard feelings towards Morgan and her child, how would they ever be a family?

Morgan was happy about the wedding because she would be able to live in Melanie's house on her own with Noah because Melanie would move in with Ron when they got married. Morgan had already picked out furniture and was just waiting to have the place for her own.

The wedding was all planned, and Melanie waited nervously for her wedding day. Ron told her she would be a beautiful bride and said he was counting the days.

Two weeks before the wedding, Ron was at Melanie's house for dinner. Morgan was there and had brought Noah downstairs while she ate dinner with Ron and Melanie. He was quietly sleeping on a blanket nearby as they ate dinner. Morgan was talking about her school work and how interesting nursing school was. Ron seemed barely interested, but Morgan was excited, and Melanie doubted if her daughter even noticed. They had just finished eating when the doorbell rang, scaring Noah, and waking him up. Morgan picked him up and went to answer the door before Melanie could get out of her chair. Morgan came back to the dining room with Ron's best friend, Mark Jones. Mark had stopped by to ask Ron if he could borrow a trailer to move some furniture for his daughter, who was starting college next week.

Morgan was still standing there with Noah when Melanie saw Ron look at Noah and then Mark. Ron's face slowly turned bright red. He was uncomfortable. She realized she had never been in the presence of his friends when Morgan was around, not since Noah had been born. They spent time around her family and friends, but never his.

Morgan seemed to put two and two together, excused herself, and went up to her room with Noah. After Mark left, Melanie got up to clean the table. Ron started helping with the dishes.

"I can do it," she said coolly.

"I don't mind helping," he said.

"I know," she answered. "It's only a few things for the dishwasher. I'll do it." She took the plate from his hand and looked at him. Ron didn't say anything, but he let go of the plate, went into the den, and turned on the TV.

Melanie worked in the kitchen, her mind going a million miles a minute. Her feelings were hurt, and she knew Morgan's were, too. After calming herself, she went into the den, where Ron was watching TV. Melanie turned it off. "We have to talk," she said seriously.

"Okay, about what?" Ron asked innocently.

"About us, about Morgan, and especially about Noah," she answered, looking him in the eye.

"What about them?" he asked.

"Oh, come on, Ron. I saw how you acted when Mark came here tonight, how embarrassed you were."

"Embarrassed about what?" he asked, surprised.

"About Noah!" Melanie answered, her temper rising.

"I was not!" he said defensively.

"You were, too; I could tell," she said harshly, trying to keep her voice down so Morgan wouldn't hear them. "Your face turned red!"

"You're wrong, Melanie; besides, Mark knows about Noah," he said trying to reason with her.

"I know that," Melanie shot back. "But knowing it and seeing it are two different things. You are ashamed of my family!

My grandson!" she said, bursting into tears. She covered her face with a throw pillow, embarrassed by the tears.

Ron took the pillow from Melanie's hands and looked her in the eye. "I am not ashamed of them," he said sincerely.

"Yes, you are," she said, tears starting to run down her face. "Yes! You are! Plus, you treat them bad."

His eyes opened wide, and he pulled his head back to look at her better.

"What kind of future do we have together if you are ashamed of my daughter and grandson?" she asked.

Ron looked at her as if he didn't know what to say. He was shocked she felt this way. He'd had no idea. He put his hands on her shoulders and shook her gently. "Look at me," he said firmly. "I am not ashamed of Morgan and Noah; I love them because they are a part of you. If for any reason you thought I was, I'm sorry. I wouldn't hurt you for anything," he said gently.

"You did hurt me, and worse, you hurt Morgan!" she said. "Your feelings are written all over your face. When Mark was here, you were nervous, as if you were guilty of something."

"Melanie, I apologize, but you're really making something out of nothing," he said.

Melanie lashed back. "Even Morgan noticed it. Why do you think she left the room with Noah?" Melanie asked loudly, glancing up the stairs to see if Morgan was anywhere in hearing range.

Again, Ron was shocked. "I don't know why she left. I thought it was because Noah was crying or something," he said.

"He wasn't crying!" she said. "Couldn't you have introduced us to your friend? Or weren't we good enough?"

"You've met Mark before," he answered.

"Morgan hasn't. Doesn't she count?" she shot back, watching his every expression.

Ron was speechless. "I'm sorry, Melanie. It really wasn't anything to get this upset over," he said after a few moments.

"Maybe not to you," she answered coldly. Melanie stood up. "I think you better go home and think this marriage deal over."

"Melanie, listen to what you're saying," Ron pleaded. "You're accusing me of something that's not true. I know what I want," he said. "It's you and all that comes with you."

"I'm a package deal, Ron; that's the way it is when someone's been married before and has children by another man. If you can't accept them," she said, pointing upstairs, "you can't accept me. Now you need to go home so I can check on Morgan."

"I'll go, but if I did hurt Morgan's feelings, tell her I'm sorry," he said, shaking his head and looking down as he walked towards the door. "I would never hurt them; surely you must know that by now."

"And by now you must know I'll do whatever is necessary to protect them," she assured him.

Ron read between the lines and looked hurt. "I'll call you in the morning," he said softly, reaching for her. He pulled her close and looked her in the face. "Don't let this destroy us," he said. "I love you too much to lose you."

"I love you, too," she said sadly.

Ron kissed her gently on the lips. "I'll call you in the morning, sweetheart," he said, looking down at her.

Melanie nodded, too drained to say much more. "Okay," she said quietly.

Ron hugged her tight. "I love you," he said, kissing her head as he held her close. He let go and backed away. "Goodnight, sweetie."

Melanie shut the door behind him and leaned against it. She was more confused than ever now. Had she over reacted? Had she imagined more than there was? She wasn't sure anymore.

Melanie went upstairs to check on Morgan and Noah. Quietly, she opened the bedroom door and peeped in. Morgan was asleep, and Noah was lying in his crib quietly looking around with an occasional gurgle. He appeared to be talking to the animals on the crib mobile. He'd smile, then he'd gurgle a little more, and then he chuckled and then more gurgling. Melanie watched a few minutes, enjoying his baby innocence. She tiptoed over to the crib and picked Noah up. Quietly, she sat down in the old rocking chair beside the crib. If this chair could talk, she thought. It had belonged to her daddy's mama. She had birthed fifteen children. Whew! Melanie thought with a smile. Noah looked up with his big brown eyes and smiled at Melanie. Gently, she started to rock him. She held him close to her chest and started to sing softly to him. Noah welcomed the attention; he laid his head quietly on her chest and listened as she sang "Rock-a-bye Baby" very softly, so as not to wake his mommy. Melanie's heart melted as she felt his sweet innocence snuggle up close to his grandma. Her eyes filled as she held him and rocked him. For a few moments, they just looked at each other, each taking the other in. Noah watched Melanie's face as the tears overflowed and rolled down her cheeks, and Melanie watched Noah's sweet, innocent, undoubting trust. Noah watched Melanie's lips as she sang to him, and then he watched her eyes as his eyes got heavier and heavier. He enjoyed the attention and tried hard not to shut his eyes, but sleep came easily and his body relaxed in her arms.

Melanie kept rocking softly, holding his little face up next to hers. She kissed him gently on the cheek. He smelled clean and fresh as if he'd just had his nighttime bath. She could smell the baby powder, and for a moment wished Kevin and Morgan were babies once again. Melanie had done that a lot, lately— wishing she could go back and start over. She would do so many things differently. Melanie took another deep breath of Noah and kissed him on his cheek softly before lying him down in his crib. Melanie was sure to lay him on his back. Morgan was adamant about that since all she had read about SIDS.

"You have a wonderful mommy, little fellow; she loves you more than anything in the world," Melanie whispered to the sleeping baby. She gently took his little hand in hers. "Grandma loves you, too, with all her heart. Nobody will ever hurt you if I can help it, and that's Grandma's promise to you."

Melanie pulled the soft blanket up around Noah and kissed him again before going over to check on Morgan, who was still asleep. She was exhausted from school and taking care of Noah. Melanie took the blanket and pulled it up around Morgan then leaned over and kissed her gently on the head. "The same promise goes to you, too. I will never let anyone hurt you if I can help it." Melanie hesitated a moment, thinking of what had just transpired with Ron. "Not even the man I plan to marry."

Melanie tiptoed out, quietly shutting the door behind her. She went to her room to undress for bed. What was supposed to be a quiet dinner at home with Ron and Morgan had become an exhausting ordeal. It had been emotionally draining, and she was tired. Her time with Noah had helped relax her. She smiled, thinking of Noah's big brown eyes.

As Melanie went to undress for bed, she caught a glimpse of her wedding dress hanging on the closet door. It is a beautiful gown, she thought. I sure hope I get to wear it. She walked to the closet door, took the dress down, walked over to the full length mirror, and held it in front of her. The gown suited her perfectly. It was floor-length, with a train, and it was snow white. Everyone said that was okay for second weddings nowadays. It was strapless with a full, flowing skirt. It was the only gown she'd tried on and she'd fallen in love with it. There were no second thoughts; it was the one. If she could only be as sure about the groom. Melanie smiled. She didn't have a sign about the wedding dress, and she was sure about that. Melanie looked at herself in the mirror. "Mirror, mirror on the wall, who's the fairest of them all?"

Melanie smiled at the bride in the mirror. The bride smiled back sadly. "Mirror, mirror on the wall—show me a sign!" Melanie chuckled at her silliness and hung her wedding dress back over the door. "There's not going to be a sign, dummy. Get over it." Joan was right; she was still asking for a sign.

Melanie didn't care, she decided to keep on asking for a sign until she said, "I do." After that it didn't matter, unless it was just to confirm she did the right thing. If not, she didn't want to know. Melanie got in bed and said her prayers as usual, but this time, her last request was, "Please, dear God, show me a si—" Then she was fast asleep.

Melanie never mentioned the incident with Ron and Mark to Morgan. She didn't want to stir things up by letting Morgan know she had noticed Ron's strange behavior. Melanie convinced herself she had overreacted and decided not to mention it again to Ron, either.

Ron tried harder over the next few days to talk to Morgan more and even spoke to Noah a couple of times. Melanie knew he was trying. She was trying, too, to put all doubt aside and concentrate on the wedding. She was getting excited, but her nerves were a mess. She couldn't decide if that was because of the excitement or because of the uncertainty of it all. She chose to believe it was the excitement. Still, there had not been a sign like she prayed for every night.

Morgan was excited because she was going to be able to live in Melanie's apartment alone when her mom moved out. Melanie had overheard Morgan telling Daryl about it and that he would be able to come over and visit Noah when he wanted.

"That ought to make the all-white neighborhood happy," Melanie thought bitterly. She felt a little guilty that Daryl hadn't been over except when she wasn't there since Noah's birth. She honestly didn't mind if he came over. Unfortunately, Melanie played the game "out of sight, out of mind," only Noah was the spitting image of his daddy, just a lighter shade.

Melanie truly loved Noah and wouldn't trade him for any child any race, but for some reason, she still had a hard time accepting Morgan's relationship with Daryl. Melanie thought it was mostly because she always worried about what other people thought about her and her family. She knew she shouldn't have to explain or apologize to anyone, but she'd always wanted other people's approval. She had always been that way. When Morgan got pregnant and had Noah, it was a challenge for Melanie to balance her friends, her family, and to stay balanced herself.

Daryl's family had a problem with the relationship just as much as she did. At first they wouldn't have anything to do with Noah, but they had since decided they wanted to know their grandson. She had overheard Morgan and Daryl arguing on the phone when he wanted to pick Noah up and take him to visit his family but hadn't invited Morgan to go along. Morgan was very protective of Noah and hadn't wanted to let him go without her. She finally agreed, knowing his parents had a right to spend time with their grandchild and wanting Noah to grow up knowing he was loved by both families. Morgan had only seen them a couple of times when she picked Daryl up at his house, but they never invited her in. His mother had been very cool towards Morgan the few times she had been in her presence. Obviously, they were not fond of their son's interracial relationship. She'd heard Morgan crying on the phone a couple of times lately and knew things were not going well between them. Maybe when she got married and moved out, Daryl and Morgan could spend more time together and not have to worry about their parents. All the negativity of their relationship had put a strain on them. She felt sorry for them, but they knew how it was going to be when they started sneaking around. Still, her heart did hurt for them. She wanted them to get along for Noah's sake, and she knew Morgan loved Daryl. She was just afraid love may not be enough.

Chapter Twenty-three

It was the day before her wedding, and Melanie had a bad case of nerves. She spent most of the day crying off and on. She had lots to do and had made several trips to town to pick up different things. Each time, she was overwhelmed with tears and had to come home to repair her tear-streaked makeup.

Melanie had called Joan a couple of times that morning, crying. She was totally confused by the tears and not sure how to handle her nerves. Each time, Joan would listen patiently as Melanie went through the same uncertainties and reassured herself it was just nerves and hung up. Joan listened, but didn't offer any advice. Melanie would go out for another couple of hours and come home and call Joan again crying, go through the same spiel, hang up again, and continue with her last minute wedding plans.

Morgan had picked out some furniture and wanted Melanie to stop by while she was out running errands, make a payment on it for her, and ask about delivery. Melanie had been too nauseated to eat anything and was feeling a little lightheaded when she stopped by the store. She was sure she looked a sight with her red nose and swollen eyes. She looked in the car's rear view mirror and wiped away her tears before getting out of the car.

Melanie walked into the store, avoiding eye contact, hoping no one would notice her slightly smeared mascara. She'd tried to fix it in the car, and her efforts had helped, but she still thought she looked disarrayed and wanted to get in and out before anyone she knew saw her and wanted to talk about her wedding tomorrow. At the thought, she felt her eyes fill. She wiped at them again. As she walked towards the payment office, she began to feel lightheaded again. Melanie stopped for a moment to get her bearings, saw a white futon nearby, and thought she would sit down a minute until the lightheadedness passed. As she approached the futon, the room started to spin, and she felt herself going down. Just before passing out, she felt someone take hold of her and lift her up.

When Melanie came to, she was lying on the white futon. As her eyes slowly focused, she saw the most captivating brown eyes she had ever seen staring down at her. His face was very close to hers, and he was sitting on the edge of the futon, leaning over her, saying something. Captivated, she stared back into his eyes. She wasn't hearing what he was saying; she was mesmerized by his intense brown eyes.

He was holding her hand. She wasn't sure where she was or why this man was so close to her or why he was holding her hand. He smelled good. He smiled, and she noticed how white his teeth were. For a moment she thought she was in heaven and this was her guardian angel. She remembered someone's arms going around her and picking her up. Maybe he was her guardian angel, and if he was, she appreciated that he was pleasant to look at.

"Miss?" he said softly. "Are you okay? Do you need me to call 911?" He was still leaning over her, holding her hand.

Melanie's heart pounded, and she felt her face flush as he leaned over her.

"Are you okay? You look a little flushed and your hands are sweaty."

He had the most beautiful brown skin. A thin, narrow mustache ran perfectly above his lip and across his chin and then up the sides of his jaw into his hairline. His hair was cut short, and he appeared to be about six feet tall. He was wearing a light yellow shirt and a brown designer necktie that complimented his complexion.

He leaned a little closer, and Melanie's heart pumped harder and faster. It felt as if it was going to jump right out of her body. Her face felt very warm, and she felt her hands getting clammy.

"Miss, I'm worried about you. I think I should call 911. Your face is really flushed."

Finally Melanie was able to speak. "No. No, I'm fine," she said, hardly able to speak.

"Are you sure? You sound a little short of breath."

"Yes, I'm sure." She still couldn't take her eyes off his.

For a moment, neither said anything. He just held her hand and leaned over her, watching. He felt her forehead. "You're warm."

"I know," she answered. "But I'm okay, really."

"Okay, if you are sure," he said concerned. "Here, let me help you sit up."

He put one arm around her waist and one around her shoulders, and she sat up. Her heart pounded as his arms went around her.

"Ready to try to stand up?" he asked gently. "Hold on to me," he said. "You may get dizzy, and I don't want you to fall again. You nearly scared me to death," he said, smiling again.

Melanie took hold of his arm and slowly stood up. She was so aware of his touch. She didn't understand what was going on. He was simply helping her to her feet, nothing more, yet she felt excited. For a moment, she felt dizzy and started to wobble. His arms went around her again; simultaneously, her arms went around him to steady herself.

"Hold on for a moment until you feel steady on your feet," he said, looking down into her flushed face.

Melanie leaned against him and felt herself getting weak. He held her tighter against him as he tried to steady her. Her face leaned against his chest, and she noticed again how good he smelled. Melanie relaxed against his body. He held her close for a few minutes, waiting for her to feel steady. A couple of store clerks came up to see if they could help.

"She's okay," he said, still holding her. "She just got a little dizzy."

The clerks seemed satisfied and walked away.

Melanie held on, and so did he. Shoppers looked at them with curiosity, but Melanie didn't care. They stood in the middle of the sofa section with their arms around each other, her head against his chest. After a few moments, he began to release his hold on her waist, and she did the same. He held her for a moment longer, but not as tight as before. After a few more seconds, he pushed away from her, still holding her lightly, and looked at her.

"I'm David, the store owner," he said, smiling. "I would shake your hand, but I think we're past that."

"Melanie," she said, softly returning his smile.

"Nice to meet you," he said.

"You, too," she replied, looking again into his seductive brown eyes.

He backed away from her still holding her waist. "Do you need to sit down again?"

"Probably so," she said.

"Hold on; I'll help you to my office, and you can rest there until you feel better."

Melanie held onto his arm and walked with him to his office. David led her to the chair behind his desk. "Here, this is more comfortable than the straight-backed chair."

"Thank you."

David turned Melanie loose and she slowly let go of his arm. He took a seat in the straight-backed chair and watched her. "Are you going to be okay?"

"Yes, I'll be okay. I just haven't eaten anything today."

He smiled. "And why is that?"

Reality hit Melanie again as she thought of her wedding day tomorrow. Her eyes began to fill with tears, and before she knew it, she was spilling the whole story about Ron, her wedding tomorrow, Morgan, and Noah. She couldn't stop talking as the tears ran down her face. David got up and handed Melanie his handkerchief to wipe her eyes. He listened intently with compassion, asking a question now and then about how she felt and what she wanted. After Melanie finished telling David her trauma, she started to laugh, wiping tears at the same time.

"I guess you didn't know you were going to meet such a nut case today," she laughed.

"You are far from a nut case. You have every reason to be concerned. If he truly loves you, he will understand, and if you don't get married tomorrow, he will wait until you are ready."

Melanie smiled, wiping tears with David's handkerchief.

"He is a very lucky man, whether it is tomorrow, or next year," he said.

Melanie smiled. "Thank you so much for letting me vent. I needed a shoulder to cry on."

"You can cry on my shoulder any time," he said, looking into her eyes and grinning again.

Melanie was like a deer caught in headlights, she couldn't look away. She was caught up in his eyes again. What is wrong with me? What is going on here? Melanie forced herself to break eye contact and look at her hands. They were still sweaty, and she nervously wiped them in the handkerchief he had given her.

"Well, I guess I better be going," she said. Melanie stood up slowly, making sure her balance was okay.

David watched with concern, ready to catch her if she felt dizzy, but the lightheadedness had passed and she was okay.

"Many things to do before the wedding," she said, laughing nervously. Again, tears filled her eyes.

David came around the desk. "May I?" he said, stopping and spreading his arms for a hug.

Without hesitation, she smiled at him. "Yes, you may."

Gently, he put his arms around her to give her a hug. This time, it was like a buddy hug. Support hug. Wish-you-the-best hug. But then she felt his hug tighten, and within seconds, her heart was racing and her face began to flush again. Melanie leaned against him one more time and inhaled his scent. After a moment, he let her go, and she walked towards the door.

"Let me walk you to your car," he said. "I don't want you passing out in my store again. You might find reason to sue me if you get hurt," he said, grinning.

"Not hardly," she replied. "If you hadn't caught me, I probably really would have gotten hurt."

He laughed. "Well, it was my pleasure to save you."

"More than you know," she said, smiling sheepishly.

When Melanie got to her car, she stuck out her hand to shake his hand. David took it and held it.

"Good luck, Melanie, whatever you decide to do. My advice is simple," he said, looking deep into her eyes. "Follow your heart."

Melanie nodded slowly, her heart more confused than ever. "Thanks," she said.

"And if you ever need a shoulder again, I'm here," he said.

She nodded, looked up at him, and smiled. Melanie got into her car and backed up. David watched as she drove off. Melanie glanced into the rear view mirror. She could still see him, and suddenly her heart started to pound and a warm sensation swam over her body. Her face flushed again.

Her hands became wet on the steering wheel, and she realized she still had David's handkerchief in her left hand. Slowly, Melanie lifted the handkerchief to her nose to smell his cologne. Her heart pounded harder. Melanie drove home in a daze. She couldn't stop thinking about the good looking stranger that had flustered her. She picked the handkerchief up and held it to her nose again, inhaling his scent. She could not get him out of her mind.

When Melanie got home, she decided to call Charles and get his opinion about her pre-wedding jitters. Maybe he would tell her what she wanted to hear. Joan had been happily married to Steve for eighteen years and couldn't relate to second-time-around marriage jitters like maybe Charles could. He had been married a second time; she was sure he had gone through the same last-minute doubts.

Melanie was sure it was just nerves. When Charles answered the phone, they talked a few minutes about minor things, and then Melanie hit him with the big question. "I have a question," she said casually, like it was nothing.

"What is it?" he asked, laughing at her for being so mysterious.

"When you got ready to marry Carol, were you unsure of yourself? Did you have second thoughts?" Melanie knew the answer before he even answered it. Everyone was bound to have doubts the second time around.

"No, I didn't," Charles said, without taking a moment to think about it. "I knew it was what I wanted, and I didn't have any doubts whatsoever."

Melanie's heart dropped. That was not what she expected to hear. She was more worried now than before.

Charles went on. "It was the happiest day of my life when I married Carol, and I haven't regretted it for one minute since then," he said, laughing at Melanie's question. "Why?" he asked. "Are you having second thoughts?"

"I've just had a bad case of nerves today," Melanie said honestly, her voice quivering a little. "I'm sure that's all there is to it."

"Probably," Charles said. "But you better be sure," he advised.

"I know," she said, trying to laugh about it like it was a joke.

Melanie talked a few more minutes and hung up the phone. She thought about what Charles had said and was more frightened than before she called him. Who wouldn't be happy with Carol? Everybody loves her; she's sweet, kind, compassionate, and a perfect match for Charles.

Melanie thought a minute and dialed Joan's number for the umpteenth time today. When Joan picked up the phone, Melanie started to cry as she told her about her conversation with Charles and the fact he never had pre-wedding day nerves. Joan listened patiently until finally, after listening to Melanie cry all day and being pushed to the point of having to give her opinion, even though she really didn't want to, Joan said sternly, "I am not going to tell you what to do, but you know in your heart the answer."

At that moment, it hit Melanie. I know in my heart the answer. I cannot marry Ron. Suddenly, Melanie felt a weight lift off her shoulders; she would not be getting married tomorrow. Melanie thanked Joan for listening once again and hung up the phone; she had to talk to Ron. The wedding was off. Melanie breathed a sigh of relief. She had known the answer all along, but hadn't wanted to admit it. That's why she kept asking for 'a sign'. Then Melanie gasped. She put her hands to her mouth and her eyes widened at another frightening thought. She had seen 'a sign' as plain as the nose on her face. A sign just like her grandmother had told her would happen when she met her soul mate—but it couldn't be. She tried to erase the thought, but it wouldn't go away. She thought about what had happened earlier in the day at the furniture store.

"No," she said, shaking her head. "No! No! No!," getting louder with each no, but it was no use; the feeling was undeniable.

David Price's face flashed clearly in her mind—his smile, his smell, his...touch. Her eyes widened more. "David Price is black!" She reminded herself, again talking out loud as she nervously paced her bedroom, trying to put things in perspective. "It would never work, and what about all the grief I gave Morgan?" She waved her hands in the air. Melanie had told Morgan over and over again she could just have easily fallen in love with a white boy and made her life so much simpler. She remembered telling Morgan, "There are millions of white boys to choose from. Why did you have to fall in love with a black guy?"

The conversation was very vivid in Melanie's mind. She had scolded Morgan for getting involved with Daryl, simply because he was black. And now look what was happening to her. Was God playing a trick on her? She sat down on her bed, staring into space as it all played back in her mind—her pounding heart, her sweaty palms, her flushed face. All 'the signs' were there, but she had not put it together until now. Melanie looked through her purse and pulled out David Price's handkerchief. She put it to her nose and smelled it again. Her heart started pounding wildly, her face flushed as the warm sensation again swept over her body, confirming her fears.

"Oh, my God," she said out loud. "David Price is 'the sign'." Melanie fell back on the bed.

She knew in her heart he had felt it, too. Would she do as David had said and follow her heart or continue to follow her lifetime beliefs?

David's smile and gentle touch burned in her memory. She smiled at the thought of him as she pulled his handkerchief to her face, rubbed it gently across her cheek, and then to her lips. Her heart pounded uncontrollably, and the warm sensation returned again as she reminisced about the tall, dark, handsome stranger that suddenly turned her world upside down and brought her 'A Sign' so clear she could never deny it, nor did she want to. Melanie knew her world was about to change forever as she crossed the forbidden line to pursue her God given 'sign' in search of her true soul mate ___ David Price.

Beyond Black and White

Chapter One (page 1)

*M*elanie woke up the morning of her supposed-to-be wedding day unreasonably happy. She had called off the wedding one day before she was to wed Ron Whitley, and instead of being sad and depressed, she felt lighthearted and free. Melanie's good friend Rebecca was bringing the wedding cake to Melanie's house, since there was not going to be a need for it at the church reception hall. She heard Rebecca drive up in the driveway and went outside to help her with the cake. Melanie smiled cheerfully when Rebecca stepped out of the car. Rebecca stared at Melanie for a moment, not sure how to act. Seeing Melanie so upbeat, Rebecca started to laugh.

"What happened since I saw you at work on Thursday when you were still planning your wedding."

"It's a long story," Melanie said, not wanting to get into all the details. "But for the most part, it was just a gut feeling I shouldn't marry Ron."

"Oh, and your gut didn't tell you this until the day before the wedding?"

"No, it told me before then, but I wouldn't listen. I kept thinking about it, though. I believe that old saying, and I'm glad I do."

"Okay," Rebecca said. "I've known Ron a long time, and he is a nice guy, but hey, you have to do what makes you happy."

"He is an extremely nice guy, and I wish him the best. It just won't be with me. He'll find someone else; the right person will come along."

"And what about you?" Rebecca asked.

"I don't even want to think about a man right now," Melanie lied, knowing there was already a man that had touched her soul like no other man ever had.

Melanie flinched at the thought of David Price and the incident in the furniture store. She had pictured his face and his smile and felt his closeness in her mind constantly since he caught her in his arms. All the signs her grandma had told her would happen when she met her soul mate happened when she looked into David Price's eyes. When she awoke, she was lying on a white futon and David Price was leaning over her, holding her hand. She was captivated as a warm sensation swept her body and her heart pounded uncontrollably. Melanie had gotten the sign she had always asked for, and now that she had it, she didn't know what to do with it. Melanie pictured his face, his thin mustache surrounding the most seductive smile she had ever seen. Meeting David had caused her to question everything about herself, her beliefs, and her future.

Beyond Black and White is the sequel to *Skin Deep*. Look for it in bookstores soon.